A
Two Summers

To Katie,

Shar...
BBC June
2014

A Year of
Two Summers

Shaun Levin

www.fiveleaves.co.uk

A Year of Two Summers
by Shaun Levin

Published in 2005 by Five Leaves,
PO Box 81, Nottingham NG5 4ER
info@fiveleaves.co.uk, www.fiveleaves.co.uk

Five Leaves gratefully acknowledges
financial assistance from Arts Council England

Printed by Russell Press in Nottingham
Design and typeset by Four Sheets Design and Print

ISBN: 0 907123 71 6

Cover images are details from "Yayati" by Bhupen Khakhar,
reproduced courtesy of James Kirkman and Timothy Hyman

Acknowledgments

"A Year of Two Summers" was first published in *Kunapipi: Journal of Post-Colonial Writing*. "That Summer Before the Army" was first published in *My First Time, Volume 2*. "After the Jahiliyya" was first published in Hebrew in *Mozna'im*, and then in very different form in *Stand*, and later a revised version in *Harrington Gay Men's Fiction Quarterly*. "Luscious Fruit" was published in *Queer View Mirror 2*. "Shoes" was first published in *The Evergreen Chronicles* and then in slightly different form in *The Slow Mirror*. "Nine Lives" appeared in very different form in *Does the Sun Rise Over Dagenham?* "The Death of Others" appeared in *Harrington Gay Men's Fiction Quarterly*. An earlier version of "A Born King of Something" was published in *Bad Jobs*. "The Good Outside" was published in *Venue, Issue 4* and later in *Modern South African Stories*.

Thanks to Arts Council England for their support.

for my family —
Ma, Dad, Robert, Laura, and Karen

CONTENTS

*It was a good place to come from
in that it was a good place to leave.*
Robert Mapplethorpe

EVERYTHING IS LIKE SWEETS

I remember stealing into the kitchen from the garden, through the side door, my mouth still tasting of blackberries, past Beauty at the ironing board ironing my grandfather's shirts and hankies. I remember creeping in on tiptoes until I was standing behind my grandmother's bum and going "Boo!" and she putting her hands — sweet and crumbly from the dough she was kneading — behind her back and reaching for my chin to tickle it.

"Your throat's sounding better," she said.

"Can I have another cough sweet?" I said, trying not to swallow.

I remember that when I got back from visiting Jonathan at the hospital, where he'd just had his tonsils out — my Auntie Edie had taken me there after school, then brought me back to my grandmother's while my mother was at bridge — I'd complained that my throat was sore.

"Jonathan said ice cream is good for your throat," I said. "Jonathan said he's only allowed to eat ice cream. With jelly."

Jonathan this, Jonathan that; I could have gone on forever.

I knew that eating would soothe the pain in my tonsils. My mother always said no when I asked for something between meals, so I put the cough sweet in my mouth and waited; I remember thinking that if it tasted of oranges it couldn't be fattening and that my grandmother knew it was good for me. I remember her squeezing the dough in the glass bowl, turning it over, then patting the lump with her open palms. The brown spots on the backs of her hands were like freckles, and there were wrinkles all the way up to the top of her arms

9

where her flesh wobbled as if it were just skin and liquid, no bones.

The kitchen smelled of melted butter and cinnamon. I remember wanting a sandwich with apricot jam and cheese. I would have asked for brown bread, not white, thinly sliced and toasted. At home, my mother, especially after a visit to the health farm, would make us eat home-baked wholemeal bread with sunflower seeds. I remember being amazed that ice cream and jelly could be good for you, the only thing to eat when you had your tonsils out. Jonathan ate ice cream and jelly for breakfast, lunch, and supper.

"Ask Beauty to help you lay the tray," my grandmother said.

And I remember carrying a chair to the kitchen cabinet to get down my grandmother's best tea pot, the silver one, and the little plates she kept for guests and for the ladies from the Women's Zionist League. I remember Beauty coming over to help, and me insisting on doing it alone, still standing on the chair, the silver tray with the ivory handles on the counter waiting for the tea pot, the cups and saucers. I liked being that high up, being able to reach everything. And when I'd got the teapot and crockery down, I opened the drawer at my ankles for the silver tea-spoons, each one tucked into a thin green felt pouch sewn by my grandmother.

"*Aai, bas,*" Beauty said, standing behind the chair.

"Isn't he a clever boy?" my grandmother said.

I remember my shorts digging into my thighs when I climbed down from the chair, my knees sticking to the padded leather seat. I knew I wouldn't have been so fat if I'd played soccer with the other boys, if I hadn't been the worst at sports in my class. I remember watching Beauty walk back to her ironing board — her skin soft, her uniform hugging her body, and then thinking about standing

10

at Mr Watson's desk with my maths homework and how, if you got your sums wrong, he'd pinch the skin at the back of your leg. I remember Beauty untying her *doek*, straightening the triangle, tightening it and making a knot in it like a bow. It was blue with tiny white dots to match her uniform.

I remember watching my grandmother roll out the dough, my chin on the table, looking through the glass bowl and waiting for her to say: "Do you want to lick what's left over?" I remember the hissing sound when Beauty sprinkled water over my grandfather's shirt and then glided the iron across it, the sound like a train stopping.

"Are you ready?" my grandmother said.

I remember her putting the back of her hand on my forehead.

"Are you sure you're okay?" she said.

"I'm fine," I said, doing my job, mixing half a teaspoon of cinnamon into a cup of sugar, mesmerised by the small amount of cinnamon it took to change the colour of so much sugar, then dipping the pastry brush into the melted butter and spreading it on the rolled-out dough, ready to sprinkle the cinnamon sugar over it.

"You haven't got a temperature," my grandmother said.

"My throat's still sore," I said.

Every Friday was the same, coming to my grandmother when my mother was at bridge, except when I went somewhere else, like when I went to see Jonathan. I remember being obsessed with Jonathan in hospital — the same hospital my father had been in when he hurt his back — and him getting to eat strawberry jelly and ice cream. I remember the cough sweet being like a piece of glass in my mouth, wanting to cut my tongue with it, but cracking it between my teeth, chewing it and swallowing it to get it safely out of my mouth.

"Next stage," my grandmother said, cutting the dough into strips, the fat of her arms swaying above the elbows.

I remember helping her twist the strips of dough and laying them out in rows on the baking tray, the cinnamon side went under and over and around. I knew that would be the sweet and crispy bit when the cinnamon twirls were baked. My grandmother opened the oven, the heat from inside like a blanket around my body as I slid the baking tray onto the middle rack.

I was hungry.

"Let's finish this first," my grandmother said. "We'll have tea and cake as soon as Mommy and Daddy get here."

So we criss-crossed the strips of pastry on top of the almond tart to create the lattice, me doing them one way and my grandmother the other. When she wasn't looking I'd put the left-over ends into my mouth, suck them until they melted and were easy to swallow.

I remember thinking that in a way everything was like sweets, everything melted and could be gulped down. I remember my grandfather walking into the kitchen, putting his book down on the table, and saying: "Nothing beats a good shit." He loved to use swear words around his grandchildren, he loved the thrill of telling us rude jokes. We always called him by his first name, never grampa. Years later, one of my cousins told me he'd grown up believing we called him N__ because he wasn't our grand-mother's real husband, although he was.

I remember my grandfather spending long stretches of time in the toilet reading Louis L'Amour. I remember my grandfather smelling of Old Spice, a smell that always makes me think of something immaculate, and his hair wet with Brylcream, his comb tucked into his knee-high sock. I remember he was on his way to the garage to fix his outboard motor and he asked if I wanted to help him.

"Go on," my grandmother said, frowning, then smiling, her particular mixture of concern and encouragement. "I'll call you when the biscuits are ready."

I remember being the kind of boy who was loyal to no-one, like a cat, settling in the laps of the ones who ignored me. That's how it was with Jonathan, my first love, a boy who didn't need any more love. I remember taking swimming lessons because he did. I remember going snake hunting because that was another way to be close to him after school. I remember once trying to get Jonathan to masturbate with me after we found condoms in his father's cupboard. I remember wanting to give him my prefect's badge because I thought he deserved it more than I did. I remember dreaming about him for years after I'd left South Africa, in one of the dreams we hid from falling bombs in a synagogue. I remember seeing Jonathan for the first time after twenty years at my cousin's wedding in LA and drinking myself into indifference.

I remember my grandfather's hand on my head.

I remember walking along the side of the house, its shade keeping that part of the garden cool. I remember my grandfather kneeling at the paw-paw tree where the last fruit of the season lay on the ground, spliting it open with his pocket knife. I remember my grandfather giving me half. I remember poking my finger into the orange flesh and licking off the juice.

"It's sweet," I said.

"How's your tonsils?" my grandfather said.

At moments it was like a swelling that wanted to burst, like an abscess, at other times it was an irritating mosquito bite. I remember looking at my grandfather's hands as he untied the ropes of the tarpaulin that covered his speedboat, the thick coarse skin, the dirt in the furrows of his fingerprints. I remember him holding me from behind

13

and lifting me onto the trailer wheel so I could pull myself up onto the boat. I remember the red and white plastic seats. I remember standing at the windshield. I remember saying to him: "I'll come help you later, N___."

"You just stay in the front, *boetie*," he said. "Don't wander around too much, or else you'll tip the boat over backwards."

I remember the excitement of being above ground, my knees on the seat by the windshield with the steering wheel in my hands. I remember facing the garage and my grandfather's outboard motor hooked onto a stand, its propeller in a drum of water. I remember watching my grandfather remove the motor's hood, check inside, then yank the starter cord until steam came out of the drum like out of boiling water. I remember how I loved to be out on the Krom River with him, speeding over the water when the sun was out and the tide was high, and we were heading for the mouth of the river, and the thrill of the choppy sea at the point where the river ends.

I remember letting go of the wheel and sitting in the driver's seat, the plastic cooling my skin. I remember the tackle box being open: bright flies, spare reels of green fishing gut, three-pronged mullet hooks, lead sinkers. I remember thinking that Jonathan had been deep-sea fishing once with his father in Knysna. I remember my envy, even though I loved the long weekends in my grandfather's fishing shack on the banks of the Krom.

I remember trying to scratch my throat with the back of my tongue and the itch not going away. I remember thinking: What if I took the tip of the hook and rubbed it against the back of my throat. I remember thinking I must be careful not to go further than my tonsils, but just far enough to scratch where it hurt. I remember trying with one finger to see if I could reach, and being startled how much closer it was than I'd he thought. I remember how

14

easy it was to scratch the back of my throat with the tip of my nail. I remember putting another finger in to go deeper, trying to breathe through my nose. I remember it being like vomiting, like when I needed to be sick and my mother would say: Stick two fingers down your throat; it'll be quicker.

I remember the bits of orange paw-paw and purple blackberries in the vomit that landed on the seat between my legs. I remember that I could hear nothing because the outboard motor in the drum was still running. I remember watching my grandfather with his back to me at the work-bench in his garage. I remember scooping the vomit onto the floor, being surprised by its warmth, and how easily it slid over the edge of the plastic seat. I remember conceal-ing it with the fishing box. I remember thinking it would dry up, like the night I peed in Jonathan's bed and covered it with the springbok skin he had on the floor. I remember the burning sensation in my throat and the sour taste the vomit left in my mouth. I remember taking a small hook and rubbing as far back as I could reach with the hook's smooth curve. I remember my grandfather calling me, say-ing it was time to go back inside, and the hook sliding smoothly down my gullet.

I remember thinking that maybe it didn't really go down and I'd coughed it up and it was buried in the vomit at the sides of the fishing box.

I remember climbing over the side of the boat, my feet dangling in the air until I found the trailer wheel and stepped back down onto the ground.

"I'm going to wash my hands," I said.

I remember my grandfather waving to me from the drum as I walked back to the house, his hands black with motor oil and grease. I remember thinking how Jonathan always had dirt under his nails and wax in his ears. I remember wishing I could have dirty ears and filthy nails.

I remember tea in my grandmother's lounge. I remember her velvet lounge suite that changed its shade of brown when you stroked the fabric against the grain. I remember my mother telling me to stop banging my feet against the side of the sofa.

"You're giving me a *shvindel in kop*," she said.

"What's with the cough sweets?" my father said.

"God, I'm eating your cinnamon thingies like a pig," my mother said.

"Nonsense," my grandmother said. "You're eating for two now."

I remember the sound of Beauty frying something in the kitchen. I remember wanting to bang louder and louder against the sofa with my feet. I remember wondering how long it would take before I made a hole in the sofa.

"Martin, will you stop it," my mother said.

"So, young man," my father said. "How's school?"

"Fine," I said.

"Std 1, hey?" my father said to my grandfather. "Can you believe it?"

"A real little man," my mother said.

"Any new boys in your class?" my father said.

"*Ja*," I said. "*Ja*, there is."

"There must be enough now for a soccer team," my father said.

"Are," my mother said. "Not is."

I remember the fire of my mother's words, white-hot like branding irons. I remember other things she said to me, throwaway sentences, handed out with a casual malice, words that are responsible for my sadistic streak.

I remember wondering whether I'd swallowed the hook or coughed it up. I remember wondering whether I should say something to my mother, perhaps suggest we go to the hospital. I remember trying to imagine where the hook could be in my body and whether it was moving around in my blood stream. I remember thinking it could get caught in my heart and not let the blood flow through my veins. I remember the drawings of the inside of the body in the *World Book* encyclopedia.

I remember there being one piece of almond tart left and my grandfather taking it and putting it in his mouth. I remember my grandmother frowning out the window and seeing two Black men fighting in the street. I remember trying to make out what they were shouting at each other. I remember everyone moving over to the window, as if gathering for a performance, and my mother coming to stand beside me. I remember her stroking my cheek with the back of her hand. I remember thinking that that's what the end of a slap looked like.

"Can we go now?" I said.

I remember my grandfather opening the door onto the *stoep* and shouting: "Hey. You. *Voetsek*" and the two Black men going silent and looking at my grandfather from across the no-man's land of his front lawn.

"Sorry, *bas*," one of them waved.

"We won't be staying for supper," my father said.

"No," my mother said. "We've got so much left-overs at home."

"Let's get the show on the road," my father said.

I remember the house being full of the smell of leg of lamb. Leg of lamb and roast potatoes. Leg of lamb and roast potatoes and peas. Leg of lamb and roast potatoes and peas and gravy. I remember how much I loved watching my grandfather carve the meat with his silver knife and the two-pronged fork.

"Are you sure you won't stay?" my grandmother said.

I remember my father looking at my mother, as if it was her call, her decision whether we go home or not.

I remember asking my grandmother who was going to make the mint sauce. I used to love picking the mint

17

from under the tap by the kitchen. I remember helping my grandmother make the mint sauce — not that night — chopping the mint on the chopping board. I remember clearly the sweet smell of African mint on my fingers, the slightly bitter taste of the leaves in my mouth.

I remember the sudden knock on the door and my grandfather going to open it, me following him, despite my mother's calls to stay in the lounge. I remember my grandfather opening the door without the chain on the latch and one of the men standing on the doorstep with a gash in his cheek. I remember the light pink colour of his flesh, how close it was to the brown of his skin. I don't remember blood. I remember him asking for Beauty. I remember that Beauty had trained to be a nurse. I remember the time she'd bandaged my head when I fell off the swing in my grandfather's garden.

I remember my grandfather saying: "You just go round the back if you want to see Beauty." I remember my grandfather's hands at the sides of his body, the grease from the motor still under his nails, his hands shaking. I remember him closing the door and us going back into the lounge. I remember my grandmother sitting on the couch putting the tea things back onto the tray.

I remember the drops of blood on the carpet by the front door when we were leaving. I remember questioning my father about the man: Was he Beauty's brother? or son? or brother? or husband? I remember my father saying that he could be anything. I remember the fear in my father's eyes.

I remember sitting in the back seat of the car peeling small pieces of dried fruit off the hem of my T-shirt. I remember thinking how when a bottle tears into a man's face it makes his flesh look like the grilled fish my father would

18

filet for us. I remember thinking of the paw paw and the roast leg of lamb and the cheek of a baby.

"Is your throat still sore?" my mother said.

"He's tired," my father said. "It's been a long day."

"I think he's coming down with something," my mother said.

"It's straight to bed when we get home," my father said.

But then, I remember there was a call from my grandmother when we got home and my father had to go back to their house. I think there'd been more fighting, and that one of the men had tried to kill the other. I remember my mother and I sitting up until late, eating the left-over *snoek* she'd bought from Cape Town airport on her way back from the health farm, eating it with Ritz crackers and drinking Milo with hot milk. I think that was the order in which everything happened, that the hook and Jonathan's tonsils and the fighting had all been on the same day, that I'd helped my grandmother make almond tart and cinnamon twirls, that my sister was at boarding school by then and that my parents were so dispassionate about our well-being. But I could be wrong.

And then years later, just days ago — after fifteen years in South Africa, and another fifteen in Israel, with two wars and three years in the army, I am thirty-two, I am in London, and I am cycling to work in Covent Garden when a truck knocks me off my bike at the point where Kingsway meets Southampton Row. I lie on my back on the pavement for a while, my bike next to me, and the driver runs up to see how I am, his face full of concern, both of us taken aback when I smile at him. The accident had been my fault and we apologise to each other. I want to hug him, to feel his body against mine. He helps me up, we exchange details, and then I go to work. Over the next few hours the pain becomes increasingly unbearable; I'm convinced I've broken a rib. Later that night in the A&E at Barts, I insist the doctors X-ray my chest, and there it is, the hook, no bigger than a thumbnail, wrapped in tissue, lodged into the side of my gullet.

THE OPPOSITE OF HOME

There have been letters in the mailbox addressed to Kenneth Laramore, or Neck Ken as we call him, asking him to give the police a ring with any information he has about illegal aliens. Meaning: Us. Isaka says he could be the one who contacted the cops in the first place to tell them where to look. She says when the police start sniffing around you stop trusting people; you pack your bags and just bugger off. That's if you've got somewhere to bugger off to. She suspects everyone, even the man who took her in and made her his lover for the past eight years. That thick-necked hunk of a man with the Barbie doll collection who's been gone for weeks without a word, leaving us to pay the rent on his half-a-house just off La Cienaga.

It all started like this: When we first came to America on holiday ten years ago Isaka was arrested for underage drinking and never bothered to pay a fine or turn up in court. My uncle, the big-shot San Diego engineer who swindles tens of thousands from his company, and who we were staying with at the time, refused to cough up the cash. He'd been bailing his kids out of jail for drugs since they'd moved to California from South Africa in the 80s, so he'd had it up to here saving asses. Isaka owes this country thousands by now. My little sister, June, on the other hand, went back to Jo'berg where she eventually got killed at a traffic light for refusing to hand over her purse. The two guys shot her while she waved her tattered ANC card at them, saying: "I'm one of you, for fuck's sake. Are you blind?" Isaka says that any country that kills an eighteen year old woman doesn't deserve to be lived in.

"Yeah, right," I say. "And what about this country?" making a sweeping gesture at her garden where cherry blossoms lie in the grass like scraps of lipsticked tissue paper.

"At least it's not ours," she says, stirring the jug of freshly-made whisky sour with a long thin ice-cream sundae spoon. "That's why here we can do whatever we want."

And we do. From the moment we got here, we've been doing more or less just that. Whatever we want. We've broken laws from day one. Despite the late great Colonel B's insistence that rules are there for a reason.

"*Ja*," I'd said. "To be broken."

"You're just a kid," he'd said, and pull me closer to him. "You still need to rebel."

Colonel B was there from the beginning, in his small white house with the big lawn, paid for by the US Army, mind you, right next door to our druggie San Diego cousins and their engineering mom and dad. For years they'd been calling him Mr B or Dr B cause that's his first name, or Mr Wells. Anything but B. Until I came along. Me, little Miss South Africa, acting all innocent, and Colonel B falls head over booties in love. Having sex with someone entitles you, plus your friends and family, to call a guy by his first name. Colonel B was strict about this kind of thing, though. From our bed one Sunday morning, after I'd moved in and become his lover boy, I heard him correcting a couple of kids who called him by his first name as he stepped out to get the Sunday papers.

"It's 'Good Morning, *Mr* B'," he said.

The canaries brought us together. Colonel B had an aviary built around the base of the sycamore tree in the corner of his backyard, which my cousins and I could see from the top of their diving board. That's where I was the day he came to the wall to ask if I wanted a closer look. We stood in front of the mesh wire watching the birds sing little birdie ditties and nibble from their seed troughs. He said he'd always loved animals; always looked after birds of some sort or another. Even in Singapore, he said, where he'd spent a couple of years, he'd fed the baby pigeons on his balcony after their parents stopped coming home.

"What did you feed them?" I asked.

"Milk," he said. "With a little dripper. On my lap. Until they were ready to fly off."

It was late afternoon and the sky was turning pink from the setting sun; the birds' bright yellow and the lawn were like those under-exposed photos. It was like this moment had now been immortalised. I was shivering, standing there in my swimming trunks; hugging myself, I could feel the goosebumps on the backs of my arms. Colonel B was wearing the tight white T-shirt he always tucked into his jeans, his black belt, his perfect moustache. His hand was warm and dry on my shoulder when he said I'd catch cold and suggested I run home and get a sweater.

"You can come back and help me cover the cage," he'd said.

Which meant I got offered a drink in the living room looking out onto the front lawn. So, what's the crime here? Well, according to the army this type of love is a no-no, and for the first year, while I was still making my way into sixteen, our love was against every bloody law you can think of. Unless you're living in Spain, or some other place where they don't have a policeman in every bedroom. Don't think badly of Colonel B; I was an accomplice in all this. His family preferred not to know, and mine were too grief-stricken over June's murder to notice what I was up to.

Colonel B was a responsible man. My aunt and uncle had known him since they moved here, and towards the end, when he could hardly lift a hand to smooth down his moustache, they even hired a maid to cook and clean for him three times a week. I'm only sorry my father never got

23

to meet him; my mother, on the other hand, said she didn't have the money to fly halfway across the world for things like that — she had a business to look after. I say we each have a grave or two that keeps us from moving around too much.

Colonel B's no longer in the picture, so there's not much point in going on about him. His secrets are useless to me; they won't drag him down when the cops finally get us, and I need the company of the living. There's nothing more you need to know about Colonel B; he was always a private person, always said there was no need to rub his family's nose in his affairs. I love him, so I'll respect his wishes. When I called his folks in Vermont in '92 to tell them he was dead, "he's dead from AIDS," I said, they said "we're coming now to collect his belongings." I took what I could and caught the bus up here. Since then I've been sleeping in my sister's spare room in West Hollywood where she'd lived with Neck Ken and his abundance of Barbie dolls, until he did a runner.

The dolls — just to get this out the way — are one of Neck Ken's big secrets (Colonel B's are not even half as strange as his). A Barbie collection does not go down well in major-league football circles. His mother left them to him when she died and he carried on collecting Barbies over the years. He says they remind him that perfection is a possibility, that long blonde hair does make you beautiful. So you can imagine the things he made my sister do with her hair and her body, plus the things he did to her when she got it wrong. He wouldn't dare have tried that shit on me.

"At least now," I say to Isaka, in the garden, still on our whisky sours. "At least now your wounds can heal and you can get a hair cut."

"I'm not getting my hair cut," she says. "What man in Los Angeles is going to look at me with some dykie hairstyle?"

"You miss him, don't you?" I say.

The point is, the police are breathing down our necks and we've locked ourselves in the house. We go out as little as possible. We're like the Amsterdam Franks and I'm little obnoxious, can't-shut-the-fuck-up-for-a-second, feelings-all-over-the-place Anna. Dear Diary. Fuck that shit. We're the hounded of West Hollywood, stealing cream cheese and smoked salmon from Pavilions on Santa Monica, plus anything else thin enough to hide under a light summer coat, whistling our way past the pungent flower stand at the sliding-door entrance. We eat the leftover fruit out of boxes at the Farmers' Market. We're the underbelly of this town living round the corner from the plump and gym-pumped of Beverly Hills.

I'd get a proper job if they'd let me. I've worked illegally and it's disgusting. No one should have to wash dishes and mop toilet floors for a living. Isaka says I'm a fat bum (which I'm not; I'm tall and skinny and look half my age) and that Ken was getting sick of me hanging around the house like a bean bag, which is probably why he couldn't stand being here anymore and buggered off. He's an active type, our Ken, not very introverted. He gets edgy when people aren't *doing* things. When you think of it, he's an accomplice in all this; I wonder if he thought about that when he went to the police.

"You should have married him," I tell Isaka.

"Marry him?" Isaka says. "I'm not colluding in some sick institution just for a green card."

"Dad's money can't last forever," I tell her.

"Oh, yes, it can," she says. "And it will."

"Let's go out for dinner, then," I say.

So we go to Bar Marmont on Sunset where we sit in the corner eating oysters, drinking kamikazes, and talking about the foreigners and filmstar-wannabes who hang out at that place. The drunker we get the more we talk about

25

South Africa and how we miss living in a big house with staircases and thick carpets, where the sea is just down the road and the waves by Bird Rock are real waves and the surfers real surfers. Our mother tells us that Port Elizabeth has become a ghost town and that anyone who's ever lived there has either left or been buried.

"LA's a fucking ghost town," Isaka says.

We're both sick of this country, but we've been here far too long to leave.

"Maybe we should move to New York or Chicago," I say. "At least it snows in winter. Nothing will remind us of home."

"I *want* to be reminded," she says. "I want to live in a place that's completely fucked up, but with great weather."

"Not I," I say. "I want somewhere just the opposite of home."

We're the only people who walk places in this town.

"That guy's make-up never runs, you know," Isaka says, pointing at the maitre d' in his high heels and frilly button-down top. "I'm going to ask him how he does it."

"He must be cold blooded," I say. "Cold blooded men have soft fresh skin."

"So that's why Ken's full of pockmarks, fur, and sweat," she says.

"Colonel B was a bit of both," I say.

"Why do you keep calling him Colonel?" she says.

"That guy at the bar's looking at you," I say. "I think we should stay away from people until this shit with the police blows over."

Isaka stirs her drink with her finger, then licks it. Her dress is the black velvet one Ken bought her from Kenzo in The Beverly Centre; it's tight and shows off lots of cleavage. She has the soft skin and perfect tits of some Japanese women. She looks at me over the top of her black framed glasses.

"Why Colonel?" she says.

"It's a term of endearment," I say.

"Fag-boy," she says. "The guy's looking at you."

"He's either a director," I say, because he's wearing sunglasses at night. "Or a serial killer."

"I think you should encourage him to come over," she says. "Smile."

The laundry room is full of Colonel B's uniforms, still neatly ironed and folded, and piles of white T-shirts. Who would have thought they could last eight years without him?

"You can never have enough white T-shirts," Isaka says.

Not long before he died Colonel B took me to Hawaii. He borrowed a friend's military passport, gave me a buzz cut, and told me to flash my tattoos as we walked through customs. I've not left this place since then. How does one get through so many years without accomplishing anything. I say to Isaka: "Leaving home was hard enough, what else is there left to do?"

Colonel B would be very unhappy to see me living like this amongst his clothes in a laundry room. He would say I should respect myself more; if you live like a bum, people will treat you like one. Old-fashioned men love the hardest; their expectations of others are insurmountable. All Isaka and I want is to survive, to get to the other end of each day and know we've spent another 24 hours away from home. The laundry room is not the worst place to be. Our great-grandparents had it worse in Bergen-Belsen; Anna had it bad in Amsterdam. At least we get out once in a while. At least we can go shopping.

If push came to shove and he wasn't dead, Colonel B would, to use his words, *save* our asses. He'd fly us somewhere, get us new identities. For all I know, he'd adopt us and make us call him Daddy. Then we'd land up fighting for his love, just like we did with Neck Ken, although Isaka has no idea what her footballer lover and I were doing in the months before he upped and left. Though if she'd poke her head round the corner she'd get a fair idea by watching me and Mr Director-Serial-Killer wam-bamming away until he splurts inside me and I fall asleep. When I wake up, hours or minutes later, who knows, the man's gone. And there I was thinking I'm about to fall in love. At least I know he's not a serial killer. If I hadn't been so uptight about keeping the house dark, keeping the sound down, keeping my cock hard, both of us might have been able to relax more, talk a bit, get to know each other. I'm sick of being dumped. I'm tired of being the one left alone. I've been thinking about giving myself in, just so I can have more people around me.

I haven't killed anyone — it's not that kind of crime — though by the amount of cash this country spends on tracking down the likes of me, you'd think I was feeding body bits to the chrysanthemums. The thing is, people like me are easier to get rid of than murderers; we have somewhere to go. Put us on a boat, a plane, a truck, and you can ship, fly, shove us back to where we came from. We're the disappearable; no need to put us in prison, or feed us, or give us medical care. Murderers, on the other hand, cost money. We're free. Free, that is, until we're caught, which, when you do catch us and chuck us out, the country becomes a much safer, much cleaner place to live in. But you haven't got me yet. I'm still running loose, lying low, vegging out in West Hollywood, waiting for your people to find my people.

A YEAR OF TWO SUMMERS

I

1978 was a year of two summers. A summer of departure and a summer of arrival.

I spent the first summer at Habonim camp in a green canvas tent on a site marked by hammocks and benches made by Jo'berg boys; big-city boys who weren't afraid to be caught smoking in their tents after lights-out. Boys proud to stand before the mirror at dawn in their shiny Adidas shorts and naked backs, still rounded and supple with sleep, shaving cream on their cheeks. Boys who had their own versions to the songs we sang and shouted them out in competition. Everything to impress.

At the start of the second summer the employment agency sent us to pick carob pods in chilled before-sunrise humidity and I had no idea where I was. They drove us in an open-back truck to the carob groves somewhere near Ashkelon. I remember Nestor's chest and small brown nipples when we sat down for lunch in the shadow of an abandoned Arab house; his thighs, thick as entire bodies, covered in hair blonded by an Argentinian sun. We sawed off dead branches and dragged them across the dew-wet ground to the open trucks, until the calluses began to bleed and then seal up and harden. By then it was time to start school again.

During the first summer questions were shrugged aside and phone-calls glided from talk to hush to: "Nothing's final yet," my father said. "We'll let you know when it's time."

And I, unable to keep the news to myself, desperate to be different in ways that forbid ridicule, told whoever I could that we were about to leave South Africa. So proud to be amongst the departing few, special at last. At the closing ceremony at summer camp I waited for my name to be called out so I could stand in line with the others going on *aliyah*. Coming to the centre, my socks caught in the barbed-wire fence around the bonfire; then, unhooking myself, I stood with the other new immigrants, SHALOM in Hebrew in fire behind us. And we all sing *Hatikvah. Kohollodbalevav pe heh ni hih ma.* Now I cannot imagine a time when I didn't know the meaning of those words, a time when I could read the prayers and not know what I was saying. You can only forget a language when you forget who you are.

And the second summer, in a world dominated by noise and uncertainty. Along the road up from the beach, rows of brown buildings chucking out music surprising in its familiarity. Stevie Wonder's real nowhere man; Rod Stewart's sailing, and the variation they were playing that summer on Beethoven's Fifth. That year I learnt the real words to *Hatikvah*: As long as inside the heart, a yearning Jewish soul, etc.

By the end of the first summer I had tasted desire in the dry, numb inside of my mouth. I had swallowed the vapours of after-rugby sweat from Christopher's body in the locker-room when Peter turned up his nose and said: "Haven't you heard of deodorant, man?" And later back in the classroom, bent over the front desk, getting caned for forgetting to bring in my Afrikaans text book, my eyes seeing only David Walker's who told me I cried as the T-rule whacked against my arse. Mr Lategan, mouth as puckered as a beak — "Budgie" we called him — takes a bunch of *vrot* grapes from his briefcase, holds them up to the class, and reminds us how important it is to eat fresh fruit, bath twice a day, live healthily. That summer the Transkei ambassador's children attended our school as honorary Whites.

At home we were told to say goodbye to Grace. I shook her hand, soft, almost melting, bleached from washing dishes. She stood at the top of the stairs, arms folded over her chest, and I cannot conjure up a memory of her eyes. I need to know now: was she crying to see me go? (And when I think that Grace might be dead now, any journey home seems unbearable.) "Bye-bye, *baas*." This I do remember: My father turns to her (their date of birth only four days apart): "Don't forget to scrub the walls," he says, "before the new master moves in."

And where was I being taken to from here?

By the end of the second summer I had tasted the sweetness of carob and fresh *halva*; I'd eaten olives, and yoghurt, and brine-pickled cucumbers; I'd turned my eyes from what they saw. In Steve's apartment on the eighth floor of Canada House Absorption Centre, Jean-Paul from Morocco taught us to dance like John Travolta. *Le fevre de samedi soir*. Night fever, night fever. We knew how to do it.

There was the summer when milk was delivered in bottles to your doorstep and you pressed your thumb into the aluminium top and licked cream from its underside. Listen to your morning cereal; put your ear to the bowl: the milk snap, crackle and popping. And the summer when we crossed the dunes and shrubs (not a *veld* anymore; a desert) to get to the shops for milk in plastic sachets that snuggled into blue plastic jugs. Snip off the corner to pour the milk onto sugarless corn flakes. No more Kelloggs. No more Nestlé. No more liquorice allsorts from Beacon Sweets.

There was the summer of fresh fruit and vegetables off the back of Mr Koopoo's van, his daughter Amshi stepping down from the passenger cabin to carry bags of mango and fresh pineapple into the house. Her long hair reaching down to her hips and the gold ring in her nose. Then a summer of rows upon rows of vegetables piled on the cement ground at the open market in Migdal (née *Majdal*, before the Palestinians got trucked out to Gaza) and the old woman with the black woollen hat and her bare-footed daughter in a red T-shirt shouting, tomatoes, tomatoes, *agvaniot*, three liras a kilo. Cheap, *be'zil ha'zol*.

And there was the summer with the thatched-roof house and the white-washed walls in Cape St. Francis. When the mullet ran in shoals like sunlight on water close to the shore and we pumped for blood worms at low-tide on the banks of the Krom River, the beach stretching from the mouth of the river to the rock pools where the waves funnelled in and washed back out, and surfers in Hawaiian shorts and brown, golden, how-could-there-be-anything-so-beautiful skin came in from the sea. That summer the hair began to sprout on my inner thighs and I shaved it off with my father's razor.

And the summer when the sea was a lake and the blue-and-white flag shivered on the roof of the lifesaver's cabin on stilts. The beach littered with tar and plastic bags and the sound of beach-bats. And life-savers, dark and hairy, tight swimming trunks like a second, taunting layer of skin. Laughing at the poor little white boy with white white skin. Hey, *kotej*. Miz Amerika. Big *tzitzi*, hey? I shaved my legs again that summer; locked myself in the bathroom to do push-ups and masturbate.

There was the summer when the neighbour was a witch with a loquat tree in her backyard. From the pool in our garden we'd throw soft fruit and loquat pips at her kitchen window; nobody dared approach the stairs to her front door. I'd rather have stolen fire-crackers from Mr Scala's than chance her evil spell. And I did — steal — on Guy Fawkes Day; David, Michael and Eytan daring me to fill my pockets.

And the summer when the neighbour was a 19-year old woman from Oklahoma who sucked on my cock for hours until I came in her mouth. There was another neighbour, too: a young Indian girl and her family from Bombay. Curry and cumin and cardamom ghosting out of their flat and filling the stairwell all the way up to San-Fransisco Steve's flat on the eighth floor. Coconut ice-cream on her birthday and a three-layered cake of vanilla sponge perfumed with rose water. And she danced for us. Enchanted, confused, lost new immigrants. Hands turning and winding to twanging music. And they were Jewish. You mean like us Jewish or some other kind of Jewish? No, all the same Jewish. We're all the same. All of us. Jewish.

But no, my grandfather wrote letters from South Africa to my father: they're hewers of wood and drawers of water. Just look in the Bible. Everyone's got his place in this grand enterprise. This kingdom.

I turned thirteen during the first summer. They were both hot and saturated with clouds of humidity, leaving no room for a cold season in between. And I longed for a winter, for a time to curl up and keep myself warm by the fireplace on the mohair carpet. There was no need for fire in the new place, this second place, it's sun so violent the sky had lost its colour. And then by December, my birthday month, the second summer was long over, and the present kept tucking everything under the mirrored surface of memory. And history became invisible.

II

It all takes place inside. I take Grace Masakele's hand and we walk through its chambers.

Africa is green, luscious wet bright green with winds and wide open sunflower fields. Travelling from the Cape up to the Orange Free State: out of the back window, crowds of round black circles in yellow bonnets. The car heading northwards as the faces follow us. We're on our way to say goodbye to family. We stop off in Aliwal North, my father's place of birth, and drive around until he says they must have torn down the house he grew up in. It's still cold outside and we swim in the sulphur baths, my father my brother and I, my vaccination for our visit to Lesotho still hurting my shoulder. Later, we sit outside on a bench eating Simba chips, cheese and onion flavour.

In Bloemfontein we play with cousins I'd never met before. My newly-found-soon-to-be-lost cousins who take us fishing at the dam and *braai* what we catch, unfamiliar sweet still-water fish. In the evenings we play *tok-tokkie*, ringing doorbells along the street, until a neighbour chases us home with his hunting rifle. "Tell your children to *pas op*, hey," he frowns at our parents, his voice carrying all the way to under the beds. "This place is full of *kaffirs*. I'm not taking any chances. "

We visit Auntie Naomi that spring. We are shown the bedroom where Uncle Max reached out his hand to turn off the reading lamp and died on the spot of a heart attack.

"Just like that," she says. "And he was gone."

We drove back to Port Elizabeth. Or did we go by train? Could we have flown? The journey home has vanished. Another black hole of memory. So I fill these holes, empty and waiting, with stories and imaginings. And when I want to give them a name I say, pain, or: nothingness. I wonder how long it is possible to stay away from home.

Back in PE my parents spend their nights packing our house into boxes. Towards the end, all that remains are beds and some paintings. The paintings will travel with us and the beds will go to the servants: my parents' double bed to Grace; a single bed to Jackson who will take it from one of our rooms to his room in Uncle Nathan's backyard where he's been living for the past fifteen years, playing poker in the evenings with Uncle Nathan and his son Leonard. Being a Shona from Rhodesia, Jackson stayed away from the Xhosa locations of Kwazakele and New

Brighton. Who would Jackson invite to sleep on his new bed? Who would follow him while he weeded the lawn on his knees in his faded blue overalls, the tight curls on his chest visible through the missing buttons as he fills the bucket with weeds and chases a little white boy around the garden with his pruning shares and gardening fork, laughing.

Grace had one or two of her own children; others had died over the years.

"Grace just had another baby," someone would say.

I try to remember what she looked like pregnant. Again: nothing. But this: she was warm; she let me be close to her body; let me watch and help her cook and do the dishes; let me eat *mngqusho* and *khubu mielies* from her plate with my fingers and put my head on her soft jasmine skin. She'd listen to me swear, *kunya*, and laugh and say, *ai-yee*, *baas*, don't let the *masta* hear you.

Over the years I'd hear how Thursday or Mary or Thando were getting along, surprised at how similar their lives were to mine, and then the stories would stop and they'd be dead.

"Grace just had another baby."

I'd go to Grace's room behind the kitchen and sit on her bed, a mountain of thick mattresses piled high to keep her safe from the *tokolosh*. The smell of hair-oil and perfume and beef scorched crisp dark brown and sweet creamy coffee in a tin cup. A smell that held out its hand and said: Stay.

Grace's son, Nelson, slept in her room every now and then, the air warm and thick with bitter-sweet vapors, and his mother in the house on her knees scrubbing floors. She didn't want him in the house. She didn't want her son to see her not his mother, but a mother bringing up someone else's children, holding little white babies who'd look into her eyes and think: You're my mother.

35

"He won't go to school, madam," Grace tells my mother.

He refuses to wear his uniform and do his homework; he insists on running around with the *tsotsies*, burning down people's houses, stealing.

"She'll have to do something about him," my father says. "He can't sit here all day. What if the police check up? Didn't we pay for his uniform and some books?"

"It's laziness," my grandfather says.

I wanted to take Nelson into the valley across the road where the Apple Express went back and forth between the coal mines in the Kalahari and the harbour at the foot of the hill. The same valley where David and I would go hunting for grass snakes under the rocks. (A couple of years ago we heard that Nelson had been killed.)

The last two months of the first summer were spent in a house with only beds to sleep on, a leather sofa in front of the television and four paintings. In one, five workers cross a field of stubble with scythes in one hand and sheaths of wheat on their shoulders, their brown skin dark against the red and purple brush-strokes of early morning sky. In another, on the other side of the fireplace, Ndebele blues and greens on the outskirts of a village. A mother and daughter lean against a willow tree on the banks of a river, the daughter resting between her mother's legs as she plaits her hair. The daughter's eyes are closed, basking in the soothing, tender pull on her skull. A dog lies beside them, asleep.

The other two pictures are in the dining room above the big round table where my mother lights the *Shabbes* candles and I refuse to wear a *yarmulkeh*.

"Must you?" my father says. "Put it on. For me."

And I do. And we watch my mother pray over the candles like a little girl playing peek-a-boo, and listen to my father saying *kiddush* over the bread and wine. And my mother rings the silver bell and Grace brings in the first course and sets the tureen of soup on a large coaster on the sideboard, by then padded and boxed and sent off to wait for us in Israel.

Only a few friends come to see us off at the airport. Next year in Jerusalem, my father says to them. We'll all be there, please God. He removes the chain with the big silver *Magen David* from around his neck and places it like a lei over my Uncle Mark's head, saying: You'll give it back to me when you get to the Promised Land. (Ten years we waited. Ten years for any sign of family. By then we'd forgotten, and had learnt, like a pack of wild dogs, to rely only on each other.)

We board the plane and my father orders a whisky.

What now? What could I have been thinking then? How do you think about something you haven't the words for? How can you think about leaving your home when you don't know what it means? How can you think about a new country, a new house, new words, when you've never experienced anything vaguely like it? So you grapple with what you have and translate it into what you see. You gradually stop thinking about the transition. You cannot be in two places at the same time, and the feelings that once looked for words begin to change their shape and take on the form of the words that are available.

The runway speeds by below us and the sound of the engine grows louder and more hollow; the plane lifts off the ground, and the noise from outside is deadened, the drone of the engine swallowed by the vastness around it. Inside there's a low hum and a lightness. In just a few hours we'll be there. Soon it will be summer again.

III

Barren land and khaki bushes along the highway. Glaring open spaces of yellow sand and towns made of blocks of

37

flats. At a roadside café, on our way to the south of the country, we stop for food. Food that until then had been exotic, bought at special shops or brought back from overseas. Humous and pitta bread, olives and cucumbers with green chillies pickled in brine. Soon to be our new daily bread. And all the signs and every sound in letters and tongues that were once confined to *shul* and Hebrew classes. This will be the summer of difference. The summer when men become beautiful. The summer when envy will barely be able to distinguish itself from desire. The summer when everything will change.

THAT SUMMER BEFORE THE ARMY

That summer before the army I cycled to the beach every morning to study for my *bagrut* exams. It was a secluded part of the Ashkelon coast three miles from where we lived. The beach was the only place I could concentrate. It was also the only place I didn't feel self-conscious about my body. Being naked in a wide open space didn't carry the same dread as being cooped up in my room without anything to ease the density of my anxieties and longings.

I'd park my bike up against a palm tree near the gravel road and strip before going down onto the beach. I'd spread my towel out on the sand, mid-way between the water and the dunes, and take out my books and notepads from my rucksack, my water and sandwiches, and then rub coconut oil onto my body. I'd sit naked, reading and taking notes, going into the water whenever the heat became uncomfortable and sweat began dripping onto the pages.

Hair had just begun to grow between my nipples. They've always been large and sensitive, which for many years meant I was one day going to turn into a girl. On the beach once with my father he showed me how to pinch their tips to make them tighten up and look smaller. But I hardly worried about being seen on the deserted beach. Only occasionally did other men come to swim, always far apart, never more than two or three at a time. Later, after Etam, I started having sex with most of the men who came there.

One was a Cuban man who asked me to lie on my back so he could slide his arse down onto my cock. He'd turn up several times a week around lunchtime until one day he stopped coming to the beach. Years later I found out that he and his wife had been deported from Israel for illegal missionary activity. Another man was the father of a boy in my class. He'd take me for rides, naked, in his jeep up the coast and we'd jerk each other off at the water's edge. His cock was shorter than mine but almost twice as thick. He asked me to fuck him once, and casually positioned himself on all fours like a man about to play horsies with his children. But his hole was too tight and my knowledge of penetration too limited. Whenever we came across each other away from the beach, he would ignore me.

Ashkelon is a small biblical town near Gaza on the South coast of Israel. It's where Samson fought the Philistines and where the legendary columns still inhabit the local park. Small towns can't keep secrets, so I was cautious when I saw Etam walking down the sand-dunes towards me, coming to stand over me to ask what I was doing.

"Studying," I said.

And I turned over onto my stomach.

"Do you mind if I sit here?" he said, sitting down next to me, removing his shoes and peeling off his socks.

"What brings you to Ashkelon?" I asked, resting on my elbows.

"Sex," he said. "Do you want to go into the bushes?"

"I can't," I said.

"Why not?" he said. "I can see you want to."

"I'm in the middle of my exams," I said. "What if I'm traumatized. Can't we meet another time?"

"We won't do anything you don't want to," he said.

"I can't," I said.

"Then just turn over," he said. "Let me look at you. I bet your cock's hard."

I pinched the tips of my nipples before turning over to let him examine me.

"You've got a good body," he said. "Do you do sports?"

"Not really," I said.

"Can I touch you?" he said. "I'll only touch you."

He put his hand on my cock and stroked it.

"Let's go up into the bushes," he said.

"But someone might see us," I said.

While he played with me, he put his other hand around the shape of his cock as if demonstrating what he wanted me to do.

"I've got my car up there," he said. "We can take a drive into the back roads."

"I'll wash myself off first," I said.

I ran into to the sea, just deep enough to rinse the sand off my skin and out of my hair. I looked at him from the water. He was brushing the sand off his trousers, like an old man. I body-surfed back to shore and walked up to where we'd been sitting. He stood with his shoes in his hands, his socks tucked into his shoes, and his beige trousers rolled up above his ankles. Sweat marks came out from under his armpits; he wore an open-necked orange shirt and had isolated black hairs on his chest and a thin gold chain around his neck.

I slipped on my shorts and T-shirt and put my books and water-bottle into my rucksack. I shook the sand off my towel and draped it over my shoulder. We walked across the sand and up into the dunes.

"Have you been to this beach before?" I asked, checking that my leg muscles were hardening with the climb.

"Quite a few times," he said.

"I've never seen you here before," I said.

"I haven't seen *you*," he said.

Through the bushes at the top of the dunes we passed the crater where sometimes I'd jerk off while watching other men on the beach. Months later a fat man in a bikini followed me up there and asked me if I wanted to be in a porn video.

"Is that your car?" I said.

"And that must be your bike," he said. "I'll give you a lift back later."

He had a new BMW, maroon, the seats soft and still cool from the air conditioning. I sat quietly in the passenger seat. He put his hand on my thigh and slid his fingers under my shorts. His skin was soft and warm against mine. I kept my eyes on the road and hoped no-one would see us. He drove the long way round, past the quarry and the old shooting range. The labyrinth of roads above the beach divided the area into a series of lots a local businessman had hoped years ago to sell to American movie-stars. We stopped in what would have been a quiet cul-de-sac.

"I've never done this before," I said.

"Are you joking?" he said.

"No," I said. "It's my first time. With a man."

He told me he was from Tel Aviv and that he sold garden furniture to hotels and holiday villages. He said he'd just come from Club Med on the other side of Ashkelon. He said he liked the idea of being someone's first time. Then he pulled my shorts down to my knees and touched my cock.

"Doesn't it ever go soft?" he said.

He spat into his hand and rubbed it over the head of my cock. He unzipped his trousers. His briefs had red, black and white stripes and the elastic band had left a furrow around his waist, an indentation like a scar.

"Take it out," he said.

The head of his cock was clay brown and much wider than the shaft. His cock looked as if it had been set in a mould: straight and smooth and hard.

"Suck it," he said.

I did. All of it. It tasted of soap and sweat.

"Play with my balls," he said. "Tickle the hairs on my balls."

His ball-sac was tight and coarse like the scales of a small fish.

"Lick them," he said.

I held his cock in my fist and sucked on his balls, one at a time.

"Oh, God," he said. "Oh, God. I'm going to come."

So I put my lips around his cock, tickled the hairs on his balls, and for the first time in my life my mouth filled with the lukewarm salty taste of cum and another man's after-shave. I gulped it down like an oyster. I read somewhere once that confusion was not a feeling in itself, that is was an excuse not to unravel and name the different emotions. At that moment I felt proud and I felt disgusted and I felt the thrill and the terror of the beginning of something.

I leaned back in the passenger seat, ready for him to suck me off. He arched his body over the gear shift and put his head in my lap. After so many years of longing and fantasising about this moment, the feel of his mouth around my cock was familiar, as if I'd always known it would be this good. I rested my hand on his head and stroked his thinning black hair. I watched his lips around my cock and thought: How am I going to tell this all to Tali? How am I going to talk about this to my mother and father when I get home? Will they smell his cum on my breath, and his sweat and after-shave on my skin?

He lifted his mouth and talked to the head of my penis: "Are you going to come?"

"I don't think I can," I said.

"Do you want me to jerk you off?" he said.

"Never mind," I said. "It'll be quicker if I do it."

He waited with his mouth over my cock as I jerked myself off, and when I came onto my stomach he licked the cum up like a duty.

"How was that?" he said.

"It was good," I said, wiping my stomach with the towel. "It was good."

"I'll give you my number," he said. "Call me if you ever come to Tel Aviv."

"I don't think I will," I said.

"You never know," he said, writing down his number. "My flatmate's about your age."

I took the piece of paper, my towel and my rucksack and got out of the car. The asphalt and the bushes were littered with used condoms, broken bottle heads that people smoked hash with, yellowed pages of porn magazines and old newspapers. I cut across the open field in my bare feet and got to my bike by the palm tree. I leaned on the padded seat and stuck my index and middle fingers down my throat. I retched and barked but nothing came out. The little bile I managed to bring up burnt the back of my throat and sharpened the taste of his cum in my mouth. I wiped the coating of slime from my fingers onto my towel and cycled away from the beach.

At home, I threw everything into the laundry basket, except the piece of paper, which I hid it in a folded bath-towel. In the shower I did what I'd seen a woman do in a film after she'd been raped: I soaped the inside of my mouth. Upstairs in my room I put Etam's number in the copper ashtray by my bed, and burnt it. Then I sprayed my room with deodorant.

"Are you coming down to eat?" my father called.

"Just a minute," I said.

I changed into clean clothes, shut my bedroom door behind me, and went downstairs for dinner.

AFTER THE JAHILIYYA

What do you expect, dear friend, of course I'm over-reacting. So would you be, on the back of an open army truck heading for God-knows-where, eyes wide open in terror, clinging to green bits and any sign of beauty along the way. Wild daisies, unploughed fields, grape vines. This is where we are: a narrow road between a mountain slope and apple orchards, suicidal Shi'ites hiding behind trees waiting to blow us to bits. I've a feeling we're not going to make it, Mario. I can tell when death is lurking nearby, when Kalashnikov bullets are about to be sprayed in my face.

Should I show you more? Do you really want to be put in the picture? Can I look straight ahead through the passenger cabin and tell you what's there? There's this: soldiers walking alongside a personnel carrier looking for landmines, like the one that blew up the truck with the officers in last week. How did I get into this? I told them I was a pacifist and they laughed. But then, quick calculation on my part, anything beats prison. So, here I am, my hands washed of ideals, ready to die before we get to the new base. People do die like this, you know, in the middle of nowhere with strangers around them. Like old men in hospitals. We never thought I'd die like this, did we? Like a war hero.

Look now. Look. From your office in Tel Aviv, watch the soldiers file back into the armoured vehicle. Watch it turn up a dirt road into the hills, heading for the look-out post across the valley from the Syrians. And look at me with my M-16 and my helmet and my metal jacket. We're on our own now, a village ahead of us, its roofs coloured by bold shades of dusk. Everything's so quiet as they wave us through the Lebanese road-block, their soldiers looking so much like us. The truck stops at a restaurant, Café Ismail it says above the door. Old men on rattan stools around low tables playing backgammon, drinking glasses of brown-green tea, indifferent to us. Two officers leap out of the passenger cabin and walk into the café. And the smells? The smells, Mario; this is a Proustian moment: succulent, crisp browned chicken skin turning on the spit. Every taste bud sits up to remember.

The farewell dinner you gave the night before I left. You made fun of me, your only friend, butch enough to fight the enemy. Was it just last night that garlic-bread-and-lasagne smells lingered on the stairs? And you made sure we got drunk quickly on the new grappa they're making on the Golan, as we passed it around the table to drink straight from the bottle. At the end of the meal — the table strewn with tin foil and dried-up bread-slices, olive pits and empty bottles — you stood up to made a speech with tears in your eyes. And we drank to the well-being of the Tribes of Israel and the Land of Israel and the Wars of Israel, may they live and prosper. Amen.

"*Yalla,*" someone shouts from the truck at the officers inside the café. One of them turns, calming the air with his open palm: *Shwaye-shwaye.* Patience.

And then London, remember? The Syrian take-away up the road from Earls Court station, near The Half Moon Bed and Breakfast. In those days when we thought we'd be lovers, and ended up being friends. The shish-kebab with chips and salad in pitta at three in the morning. We were regulars by then. You and I and the late-night revellers wandering the streets. We had plans. We were going to work in pubs like Australians and then trek through Peru and Kerala. But we got homesick, me in particular; you'd left home once, coming from Turin to Tel Aviv with your silly Zionist ideals, and so we went back. To what? To this.

A fucking war, Mario. Asthma rescued you and gave you a nice office job. Me, I'm now part of some trigger-happy army, cruising Lebanon, waiting for take-away chicken in some Druse village miles away from home.

How the mighty have fallen.

It's all so different here, Mario. It's true what they say, this is the Switzerland of the Middle East. The signs are in French and the green is the green of earth washed in melted snow. Not like that desert we come from. None of that stark sunlight, that even now in winter bleaches the sky to a barely-discernible blue. Look through the vines, you can see the lake, rippled like crystal, its shores wide and expectant as if waiting for naked marines out of some Bruce Weber postcard. Is it possible that only yesterday we were at Lola's, drinking until we'd covered the table in beer bottles? You and I alone in the pub after the others had gone home, and we'd wandered out onto Allenby Street to find an open bar. "Leave the bottles," we told the waiters, "Don't touch them. We want to keep stock of the ground we've covered."

Why did we drink like that, Mario, the way alcoholics do when they're frenzied and driven and have ready cash? I'll tell you why: we drank because I knew I was off to die. I was convinced I was destined to die an heroic death on the battlefields of Lebanon, poppies blooming after the snow has melted. These aren't just clichés, my friend, they're a reality waiting to happen. And you smiled, unbelieving as usual. "Enjoy me while you can," I said. "Humour me, be kind, because soon I'll be strewn across grassy plains, tiny red and white flowers growing from the chunks of my flesh." And you said, plucking anemones from my coat: "Wipe the spittle from your lips. You're mumbling again."

We spent our last few hours walking around the old port off Yordei Ha'Sira Street, the sun just coming up,

47

tinting the piers and turning the sea a deep blue. We must have been sober by then, me getting ready to catch the bus up North, you about to go home, clean up, wash the dishes, head off to your office at the army base in the centre of Tel Aviv. What did we say to each other? It's hard to imagine what we could have shared besides silence. We've always been good at silences, haven't we?

The two Druse soldiers behind me are singing a war song. Or is it a lament? I'm straining to catch a word, trying to get the gist of it, but my handful of words in Arabic aren't enough to make out what they're saying. One of them stops and leans forward, his mouth this close to my cheek.

"New here, are you?" he says.

"Me?" I say, turning to face him.

"My name's Muhammed," he says.

We shake hands and I tell him mine, both of us shouting through the truck's noise and the wind.

"So this is where they sent you?" he says.

His eyes are bright green, his skin so brown and smooth it exposes everything inside me. I force myself to stare into his eyes to avoid gaping at every other part of his body. I hear nothing, the way you do when you're in love, and he's talking to you and all you can do is bask in his presence and the soothing sound of his voice. And you don't really care what he's saying. Only to watch his lips move and his green eyes and his stubble, the stubble that should be licked by my tongue.

"This is my cousin Samih," he says.

"They sent me from the Southern Command," I say.

I know, just be matter-of-fact, business-like, formal, don't overdo it with the blah-blah. Don't worry about me, Mario, I know how to behave in a situation like this. And don't raise that eyebrow of yours at me. I know what you're thinking: Oh, no, not again. He's only been here five minutes and already he's in love.

"They screwed you," Muhammed says. "You should have said no."

"It was either this or prison," I say.

And I hug him to me, tuck my head into his shoulder, smell the *za'atar* and tangy goat's cheese his mother packed for him; swallow the musky flavour of his sweat; lick the saltiness off his varnished skin, and he smiles, caresses my back, wraps his arms around me.

"Poor you," he says.

"It can't be that bad," I say.

"You'll see," he says.

His spiciness lingers in my mouth while I question him about the latest incident on the western front, just south of Kefar Kook, closer to Rashayya, there, isn't it over there? Just past the sharp turn in the mountain? On and on. Anything to calm myself down.

"How are the home-leaves?" I say.

"Not bad," he says.

But I can't wait any longer. I must say to him: Muhammed, we can't live together in your village. It's not practical. We need a place where our love can grow. I will teach you everything. I'll show you how our love can last forever. See us in fifty years time, deck-chairs on the beach, me trying to hold your hand and you creeping away from me. You smile at the young woman on her towel in front of us, so aglow with suntan lotion she could be our daughter. Then at home, getting ready for bed, me under the duvet in my flannel pyjamas, glasses on the bedside table, you floating around in your white bikini briefs, folding jeans that still cling to your body. Then you unbutton the silk shirt that brushes against the tips of your nipples, and come to me, and slowly, lovingly, begin to caress me.

"I feel at home here," Muhammed says.

49

"Do you?" I say.

"I've got family here," he says.

"Family?" I say.

"*Wallah*," he says.

The two officers — I, too, had forgotten where we were, Mario, being as I am so close to eyes like his — come out of the café and climb back into the truck. Muhammed's friend shouts something to the cook, who lifts his head and stares at us as we drive away.

"The cook's his uncle," Muhammed says.

At the road-block on the far edge of the village, two women in black dresses sit with their soldier-sons, keeping them company, knitting green, black and red scarves. Into the darkness, and only the road ahead is visible in the headlights, until the moon appears in a large puddle of rain. The only sound is the droning of the truck's engine and the mournful singing behind me. In the distance, the chimneys and antennae of the base are illumined by a dim light; and as we get closer smoke ribbons and prefab buildings become visible. What am I doing here, Mario? Will I ever be able to share this with you, and tell you what's really going on without sentimentality or jokes.

"There's a spare bed in my room," Muhammed says.

I know, I know, I'm asking for trouble. I can see you wrinkling up your nose. I can see your let's-see-you-do-it-then smile. But I'm the one who's here, alone, with Muhammed, ready to follow him to the ends of the earth. I don't have a choice anymore, dear Mario. I'm walking across the base, following Muhammed with my kitbag and my ammunition-pouch and my lance of chivalry. And I'm thinking: I'd reconquer Spain for you, my love. I'd slaughter the infidels with my bare hands. I'd prepare our victory feast of mutton in goat's milk. I will be your bard and suppliant.

"We'll be in time for the midnight snack," Muhammed says.

The dining room is heated, the air heavy with paraffin fumes. Eight tables, two occupied, all have loaves of sliced bread and tubes of strawberry jam on them. Heads turn. Muhammed introduces me to the soldiers at the table next to ours, and I think to myself: At least I'm not the only Jew here. The cook brings a pot of steaming black tea and welcomes me, laughing. A brief exchange with Muhammed and he goes back to the kitchen.

"A cousin of mine," Muhammed says. "I brought him some stuff from home."

I spread margarine onto a slice of day-old bread and squeeze out thick red jam, then cover it with another slice. I wash down the sweet, velvety taste with strong mint tea. Muhammed fills me in about the base and about his brother, who didn't join the army and came to study religion here in Lebanon. I stare at the triangle of naked skin made by his top button and the two folds of his collar. I glide three fingers along his neck and stroke soft skin. I'm losing my breath as I undo the first button then another to enlarge the triangle, another, until a narrow rectangle of skin stretches from his belt, past the delicate hair around his belly-button, over his chest, and up to his throat.

"Are you coming?" he says.

In the room he opens his buttons alone, and I keep asking questions, hoping each story will bind him to me further. He tells me about the officers and the base commander, who's from his village in the Galilee, and about the adjutant, whose uncle's a member of the Knesset. He tells me that if war breaks out between Israel and the Druse, he'll go over to their side. He folds his shirt, lays it down on a faded crate of mortar-shells, and sits on his bed to unlace his boots. Mario, I've hit the point of no return. Head over heels. Don't laugh. See how he moves cross the room to light the kerosene heater with a match; the way he unfastens his belt; and, as if he were alone in the room, he pulls down his trousers and bends over to take them off.

I turn to my kitbag to look for something, but the zip's stuck and there has to be something I can look for in here, has to be, and if there isn't I might just land up doing something silly like going down on my knees with my mouth wide open.

"Is everything okay?" says Muhammed, spreading out his sleeping-bag and blankets on the mattress, the bed-springs groaning as he sits down.

"I'm on guard-duty from two," he says. "I'll try not to wake you."

At last I've found it, ripped open my bag to offer Muhammed the small bottle of vodka you bought me at the kiosk on Yordei Ha'Sirah Street just before I went off to catch my bus. He takes it and raises it, salutes a *le'chaim*, and drinks, his rib-cage standing out like Jacob's ladder. Can you see what's happening, Mario, as he hands me the bottle and lies back on his bed, his white briefs barely hiding lush pubic hair. I need to sit down now; my mouth is dry and my knees are about to cave in, and I can't look at the thin line of hair from the top of his under-pants to his belly-button, nor at his chest, his nipples, the hair sticking out of his armpits, his deep shoulder-blades, neck, chin, mouth. A mouth that says: "I'm exhausted," as he puts his hands behind his head and closes his eyes. I am on my knees, Mario, giving thanks where it's due.

Loud knocking wakes me in the morning.

"Come on out," Muhammed's cousin says. "Come and have a look."

I don't want to know what's happening out there. I don't care about the outside. All I want is the kerosene warmth of this room, our room. Muhammed's sleeping bag lies cuddled up with his blanket in the middle of the mattress. I hadn't heard him dress or leave the room. My lover is thoughtful; he keeps me in mind. He will be back soon. I know he will. And I know, the way you know when something new is about to begin, that I'll see him night after night, the two of us brave warriors, lying across from each other, drinking vodka from the bottle, tearing off pieces of pitta soaked in olive oil and *za'atar*. Be happy for me, Mario; I have found beauty and love.

I raise myself out of bed and put on a pair of shorts. Outside, everything is white. While I slept and my lover stood guard, a thick layer of snow has encased the world. Near the flagpole, two officers in khaki vests and red paratrooper boots are throwing snowballs at each other. The sky is a perfect blue, the clouds animation white. And from the watch-tower at the entrance to the base, Muhammed walks back towards me, leaving deep footprints in the snow between there and here.

LUSCIOUS FRUIT

I tell myself to keep reading, that this is an exciting bit, an important bit, that any word missed will cause a misunderstanding of the entire plot; I mustn't skip one word, even if, by the time they get to the gate, I have to go over each sentences again and again. By the time they make it to here from the cactus plants on the side of the path, walking up from the main road, I should be on the next paragraph, I should know what's happening. Keep going. Any second now they'll be here. Don't miss a word.

"Hey, *shomer*! Do you want to suck his cock?"

I open the gates for them and let them in; they're the two cooks, Amos and Ziv. I have to find a way to look at them without them catching me. I can't let beauty, no matter how vicious, go unstudied and unappreciated. Years of being bullied teaches one to hate the torment and love the tormentor. Their perfect uniforms, fresh, pressed, loose enough on their bodies to leave room for the imagination, space for the mind to live between skin and fabric. To brush against smooth bodies. Ziv the darker one, a Tunisian; Amos an Ashkenazi of some sort.

"Amos," Ziv says. "Do the guy a favour, let him suck your cock."

I close the gates and go back to my book, Kerouac's *On the Road*, reading it in English, the language I was wrenched from just four years ago, waiting to escape from this. I read every word — "There were long, funny days in Carlo's apartment…" — concentrating on each sentence, working myself into the story, away from here. It always comes down to this in the end; just a matter of time before the other soldiers find out, then they never let go.

This is the third base I've been moved to, closer to Tel Aviv now, so I don't need to stay overnight, don't need the near-death of being in Lebanon or the boredom of manoeuvres in the desert down South. But alone here on guard duty at this time of the morning is asking for it. At least in the late afternoon there are two of us. I wait and listen now; they'll have more to say before they disappear into the kitchen.

"Not a chance," Amos' voice further away, almost at the kitchen door. "You think I'd let just anyone suck my cock?"

Amos grabs his crotch, sucks in air through his puckered lips, thrusting his pelvis out at me. Why do they taunt us with the thing we want the most? Their laughter flinging one memory after the other at me, as if I am destined to keep being sent back to primary school. Their laughter, like yesterday's laughter; the boisterous chuckle of bullies with secrets that terrify them. Who else could have done it? Not that I really care. Let's face it, not everyone gets to star on a toilet door, on an army base just outside Ramleh, or anywhere. Just me and Shosh, the switchboard operator. Shosh gives good head. Call this number...

Later, at lunch, banquet-sized aluminium trays of breaded chicken breasts and mashed potatoes, a young corporal sits opposite me, eating with his fork, which takes me back to the months before going into the army and watching Jeremy Irons visit his father in *Brideshead Revisited*, the two of them sitting in silence at the dinner table, him eating only with a fork. The young corporal is like that: Effortless. A kind of aristocrat, born into an abundance of masculinity. He's new at the base, a paratrooper, says he was injured up North. I try not to stare, try to concentrate on my food, slice my schnitzel into thin strips, stick my fork into each one, crown it with mash.

"Could you pass the bread, please?" the paratrooper says.

I slide the plastic bread basket across the table as if I was offering my hand to be kissed.

"Thanks," he says, tearing off a chunk of bread, putting it in his mouth.

"Where were you wounded?" I say.

"Near Tyre," he says, scooping some potatoes up with his bread.

But I want to know where the scar is, to be shown where on his body the flesh has been sewn together. I want to lick his skin, to search for the healing wound. To run my tongue across his chest, the salt of his stomach, the brittle hairs on the insides of his thighs. I think of the lucky surgeon, singled out by fate to pluck the bullet from this man's body.

Sima, the base commander's secretary comes over to our table to talk to the paratrooper. She tells him the commander's waiting, that it's time for him to go for his interview. The paratrooper picks up the last bit of chicken from his plate with his fingers and leaves.

Galit comes over to my table, smiling like she has just watched me perform and is pleased with what she's seen. Like we're conspiring. We pick at the cold potato mash with our forks, helping ourselves to what the paratrooper has left.

"Delicious," she says.

"Very," I say.

"I could eat the same thing every day," she says.

"And never get bored," I say.

Dana and Sigal join us. Now there are three girls at one table; apparently it's all too much for Amos, an opportunity not to be missed. He marches out of the kitchen, chest out like a peacock.

"Hey, girls," he says, ignoring, rather than including me.

Ziv is left in the kitchen with the dishes while Amos settles down, crossing his legs, his arm, resting his elbow on his knee, cigarette held between the tip of thumb and index finger. He inhales and grins at Sari.

"A little dessert?" he says.

"How little?" she says.

The laughter of young women.

"Enough for everyone," Amos says.

Sari raises her eyebrows, turns up the corner of her mouth. It's at this point that Amos puts his cigarette out in the tray of left-over mash and brings his chair closer to the table. He rests his elbow on the formica top, palm open in an invitation to arm-wrestle.

"Give me your hand," he says to Sari.

She laughs: "Pick on someone your own size," she says. "Let's see you and him."

"Fine with me," Amos says. "Let's go outside, then. Like real men."

Quick calculation: it's much safer to arm-wrestle. I'd never get anywhere in a fist-fight; I've never been good at one-on-one combat. I have at least five incidents as proof. That doesn't mean I wouldn't love to see my knuckles sail through Amos' pink face, collide like a mallet with his pug nose. I would love to see his brain trickling down the bright yellow wall in the kitchen. I am always planning my revenge.

The girls crowd around and Amos pulls up his sleeve, his skin smooth and tight, beautiful green veins running up his thick arm. And now I will touch them. A prelude to touching his hairless tummy, his protruding belly-button, that tiny foetus at the tip of the soft line of hair pointing up from his pubic hair. He clears the table: plates, cutlery, bread basket all swept aside. And I think: If only she was here to witness my imminent victory.

"Come on," Amos says. "Let's go outside."

But we hold hands, link palms. His skin is soft — like my grandmother's, I think — his fingers wrap around my hand.

"Let's get this over with," he says. "One, two, go."

Now. Push down. This is for HOMO on the toilet door. I'd gone in yesterday after lunch, crouched down on my haunches over the hole and there it was, bright red paint on the grey of the door. And it was still there this morning. Who else could have done it? Come on, down you go. And I want to call out to her: Look. Come and watch this. This one's not going to be like Ben Rosen, with his dark stubble and black eyes, jumping out of his sleeping bag to grab me, his thick hairy forearms, his fists flying. Not like that night in David's car, the other guy swerving to cut us off when he saw us kissing, edged us onto the side of the road. The young boy, a fucking teenager, waving a knife, coming up to the window. And I'm shouting at David: Drive. Keep driving. The boy's hand like a memory in my face. I didn't feel a thing, as if shame were an anaesthetic. And not like the time by the bike-shed near the *sukkah*, Joel calling me names — *moffie*, girl, mommy's boy — then pushing me while the others stood in a circle and laughed.

"Shit," Amos says, getting up, shaking his hand, moving back to the kitchen. "Next time we're going outside. Like men."

I'm at the gate again later that day, early evening when people are leaving the base. Ziv and Amos are coming down the path from the kitchen. My book's in my pocket; the paratrooper is next to me, learning the ropes. We open the gates together.

"Got your boyfriend with you?" Ziv says.

"Fuck off," the paratrooper says.

"Amos, Amos, let's give him what he likes!"

But Amos keeps walking, boots marching down the asphalt towards the main road. I watch their backs, the way their uniforms hug their narrow hips, their cute arses. And I wonder where the strength in my arm comes

59

from, and I think of me and my grandfather sitting in the kitchen while my grandmother made fudge. I think of him putting his little finger in his mouth and blowing into it, like a valve, pretending to blow up his muscle, and no matter how hard I'd push down on his bicep, his muscle would stay hard.

"Hey," Ziv calls after Amos. "What's the matter? Slow down."

SHOES

They're red leather shoes with a gold thread hugging the tip, running along the rim of the shoe to meet at the top of the pencil-thin heels. The leather is soft and smooth like the skin of a peach. The touch you can feel without touching. I imagine the leather pressing against my skin, cuddling my toes together, holding onto the sides of my feet. I imagine being lifted, head high and towering over the rest. I'm here at the window, my nose against the cool glass, watching the shoes beckon to me like an open palm, waiting for me to slide my feet in. One at a time. Slowly and lusciously like a knife into summer butter.

My hands sweat against the glass, a circle of mist around my nostrils, and my feet are so tired. Heavy like lead in these flat heels. The day began months ago, and I need to rest. I want to be able to walk into the shop and buy those shoes, and for a split second I can picture myself striding in, parting the glass like saloon doors. I'm here. Serve me.

But I can't. Not any more. People recognise me in this city.

The last time I bought shoes like this was back in high school, in the days when I could hide from the world behind family. I'd take the bus into Tel Aviv where the buildings and the streets and the hot smells were still new to me and the people all strangers. It was safe to do that then. I could tell the salesman that they were for my sister, please, or for my mother.

"Should I wrap them, then?" he'd say.

"Oh, yes, please," I'd say.

And I'd watch him cover the box with wrapping paper and ribbons. I'd watch him slide it into a sturdy shopping bag and I'd take it from him like a gift. On the bus home

I'd sit with the box on my lap, rubbing against me to the gentle vibrations, my cock getting harder as it chiselled its way into me. A sixteen-year old boy's anticipation of womanhood. The shoes were my antidote to fear and shame.

Back in Ashkelon, I'd dump the bag, the box, and the wrapping paper into a bin before going home. I'd hide the shoes in my jacket, under my arms, and go straight up to my room. Buy anything nice? my mother would call from the kitchen. Just walked around, I'd say, and hide the shoes at the back of my cupboard, covering them with the spare blanket. Each night I was surprised to find the treasure beneath the yellow, faded blanket. Each night I'd rediscover the shoes, safely hidden away like stolen goods. Each night was the same journey, each time a little closer. My first pair were platform shoes with black leather straps and thick perspex heels embedded with gold and silver stars.

Always a man of extremes, my mother would say.

I'd sit at my desk, right leg over left, the gentle weight of the shoe tugging at my foot as I nodded it up and down, up and down, like an engine revving up, like an athlete waiting for the starting gun. I'd file my nails with the emery-boards I kept in my desk drawer, stroke my long straight hair with my ivory brush. I'd eye myself in the mirror, run the tips of my fingers along my legs, down to the shoes, caress the leather that pressed snugly against my toes, hugged the sides of my feet. I'd cup the heel in the palm of my hand; its cool transparent texture like glass.

Then I'd walk slowly across the room, a white sheet draped over my body, keeping to the carpet, careful not to let the loud heels touch the floor. With heels like these you can't walk too slowly. If you don't keep moving, swaying your hips from side to side, you lose your balance. Stop pacing up and down, my father would shout from downstairs. I'm doing my homework, I'd say. I'm thinking.

I only stop now at windows with shoes for men and for women. With my face towards the crass boots and indelicate brown and black Italian shoes, I let my eyes feast on the long shining white boots and the thin heels on the slim blue, green, or orange shoes. Not shoes. There should be another word for them. They have these tiny silver studs. They have gold-tipped points. They have three little buckles, bridges over the top of the foot. I've got used to doing this. Facing one way, and looking the other. If the winds change I'll probably remain this way, squinting to the side, my face to the front, for the rest of my life. Never make faces, my mother says. The clocks strike, the winds change. There's no turning back.

I can't just walk into a store, buy the shoes, and take the nice and easy route home. The route that's green and tree-lined and no one sits on park benches and calls out to you. Hey! those beautiful high-school boys you want to look like, but cannot, will shout. They point and jeer. The sound of their beer bottles ringing, cheering: *Le'chaim*, *motek*. Sweetie-pie. Throwing their heads back to laugh and gobble down warm beer. Their hair shines in the sunlight and their tight skin, unblemished, clings to their bodies like lovers. Skin you cannot touch. You see nothing. You hold your hands tightly at your sides, your insides in your hands, and you keep walking.

It's a sunny day. The sky is blue and the sidewalks are clean. I'd walk into the shop and the salesman, nice jacket, open-necked shirt, light wool trousers would approach me, respectfully.

"Sir," he'd say. "May I help you."

"Those there," I'd say. "The red ones in the window."

"They're you," he'd say, and smile. "Would you like to try them on?"

"Yes, please," I'd say. "Thank you."

Sometimes it's not enough to do what you want in the

safety of your own home. You want to take it with you out onto the street. Sometimes you become so afraid of an open door you stop the thoughts from venturing out; you chase away the voices begging to be let in. Sometimes I think pacing up and down in my green knee-high boots and threadbare denim shorts is not real if no-one can see me. I can stroke myself in front of the mirror. I can knead my chest, push on the muscles, press against my nipples. I can pull my stomach in. I can hold my head back. I can feel my hair brushing against my spine. But it's just me looking at me.

I want those shoes. I want them like a man who wants a man cannot live without a deep voice close enough to inhale its soothing sound. I want them like a cynic longs for beauty and a joker longs for candour. High-heeled shoes carry you to such warm, strong places you cannot help but want to go back. I reach inside and touch those places. Stroke them, lean on them. I pull up my black tights and put on my silk blouse, a blouse so thin only skin can see it, the blouse that tickles the callused tips of my nipples and rustles against the stubble on my chest. I swing my hands and move my hips to a rhythm only high heels and silk garments dictate. Then I am happy.

She's standing next to me now. Could she be looking at the same shoes?

"Aren't they gorgeous?" she says.

"The red ones?" I say.

"Gorgeous," she says.

I have memories. Nice childhood memories from a childhood I prefer to forget. My mother's dressing room with tall oak cupboards and a thick cream carpet. A vanity table with a square leather-framed mirror and perfumes and pink powder with soft brushes. The wine-red Lancôme case with rectangles of blue, green and brown eye-shadow. When my mother was out, her dressing-room was mine; I could try on anything I liked: the tennis skirt with the pastel sunflowers, the skin-coloured stockings, the mink stole that even in summer was so cool I wanted to keep my cheek in it forever. I'd wrap it around my shoulders and stand before the mirror. From this void of evening dresses and soft shoes that were too big, and just right, for me, I would step out into the bedroom, flinging the skirt's hem to the sides and spinning to make a tutu around my middle.

At the vanity table, I'd brush my cheeks gently with rouge and paint my eyelids with blue eye-shadow. I'd screw the tip of lipstick out of its tube, make an O shape with my lips, paint first the bottom then the top lip, rub them together, back and forth, spreading the colour evenly, like my mother did before she and my father went out dancing at The Room at the Top on Rink Street. Then I'd hold a tissue between my lips and press down to remove excess lipstick, my mouth now full of its flavour, a taste unlike anything else in the world, a taste that is nothing but itself.

Memories like these become immortal. That's when dead things stay alive inside. But like the dead, they haunt you. They come back to trouble you with unfinished business. They take you through labyrinths of mysteriously connected threads. Everything is joined to everything: the rouge to the mirror to the white skirt to the shoes in the window. And back to Dana and the ballet classes I wanted to be a part of, and to her brother Jonathan I loved so much I wished I was Dana.

Buy the shoes, already!

Easier dreamt than done. It's not a question of money, nor a question of whether Leo would frown on it or not. He encourages me. He even bought me a satin night-gown on his last trip to London. That's proof enough. He's a nice guy. My boyfriend, Leo. Tall and dark with a beautiful chest, thick hands with long, slim fingers. From the moment we met — well, after the first few times — I told him: "This is what I like. You like it, stay; you don't, don't." He said; "You look good in that. Let's see you walk across the room."

Now I have my shoes made for me. So I must try, while I stand here, to memorise everything to take to Olga. Give me specifics, she'll say, or else you'll never get what you want. So I must remember the things that count. The size of the heel and the shape of the tip and whether the leather is matted or shiny. I like the heels to be high enough so the ground seems softer, farther away. And the tips must be round. Olga says the rounder the tip the kinder the step. More subtle. It's her philosophy of footwear.

As for herself, she says if only she looked different she'd make her own shoes. What's the point, she says. If a person's fat and ugly, who cares what they wear? Nobody notices. Unless they dress like thin people. Fat people who dress like thin people get noticed. *Davai*, come in and sit down.

Her place is like the Palace of Versailles reduced to fit into one room. For guests, a red velvet chaise-longue with a heavy wooden frame and one lace cushion. She sits in a high-backed chair where she strokes her Pekinese with one hand, her other hand waiting for instructions, ready to sketch. We drink tea from the samovar Olga brought with her from Moscow. We suck on sugar crystals, and she says: *Davai*, now tell me everything.

I have learnt not to take the small details for granted. In the beginning I would tell Olga to put the glittery stars on this side of the heel, and make a rounded point. And back at the window the glitter would be on that side of the heel, and the point much pointier. I've learnt to pay attention to what I must remember. I have no choice. I can't walk into a shoe shop, dressed in a dark suit and leather briefcase, and ask the mouth with the wad of bubble gum, do you, excuse me, but do you have those red leather shoes, the ones in the window with the golden strips, yes, those ones, do you have them in a size forty-four? And her nose becomes a raisin; her eyes — narrow slits of suspicion.

People do that here. They don't mind asking who it's for, how much you earn, how much rent you pay, or what is it exactly the two of you do in bed? I just can't imagine! It's not that I mind, they smile, it's just I can't think how you people can enjoy yourselves. If you want to fuck, the braver ones say, why not fuck the real thing.

Leo and I get our kicks out of imagining what the couple at the next table, the one with the steady jobs and the baby-sitter, would say if they saw us at home. Never mind in bed, just walking around the house. Me in my tight skirt, stockings, and high-heeled shoes. Leo in his Levi's, white from wear around his beautiful thick cock, and his brown cowboy boots, and that white vest that hugs his wide chest tighter than I can. And if they came on Thursday nights, they wouldn't know what to do.

Thursday is the day I am made into my true form; Thursday is shaving day. I lie naked on the bathroom mat and Leo lathers me with shaving foam, icing my chest like a birthday cake. His beautiful, caring muscular hands on my body. Then he takes the razor and goes gently across my skin, removing the bristles from my chest, circling my nipples, stopping to pinch them with the tips of his fingers. And like a magician, uncovers me, clears the foam with a warm towel. Then he does my arms and my legs, taking care not to touch the sensitive flesh. Thoughts of his hands so close get me hard. Now? Leo says. Now, I say. So Leo sucks my cock until I am almost about to come and my whole body is alive and ready to be fucked.

Leo lines my arsehole with Johnson's Baby Lotion, straight from the pink plastic container, then tickles the insides with the tips of his fingers. First one finger then two and then three, four five. Opening me up wider and then wider and I want to take in as much as I can to take into me that hand that is all mine. Now that my arse is open and loose and all my resistance worn away, he takes his fist out and lies down on top of me, sliding in and out with his cock. My muscles gradually contract to hold onto him, and I push myself up onto all fours and he holds his arms across my chest and kisses my neck and pulls my nipples and strokes my smooth chest and moves down to my cock and plays with it until I can't tell anymore where the sensation is coming from nor what the sensation is and I start to forget myself, to disappear into that place of nothingness, that void of pure pleasure without words. And when I'm about to come I push harder back against him, wanting to be taken away, to disappear into his perfect body, into his solidness, into what I will never be. And then I am full.

Sometimes we go out and I'll wear my high heels and stroke the long straight hair that runs down my back, and make Leo want me. Want me, I say to him, tell me you want me. Tell me that you'll die if you don't have me always. He does, because he would. That's how we met. I was the one who did the seducing; two years ago at a big Purim party in the old harbour in Jaffa, I wore my chiffon evening gown with an open back and a slit down the side. I wasn't shaving my legs then, so I had on my black stockings and the shoes I'd picked up that morning from Olga. I was perfection. I stood at the drinks table smoking a joint and waiting for the barman to pour me another Harvey Wallbanger.

He came from across the room. I'd noticed him before, but had kept his image to myself. He was the only one who hadn't dressed up. There were Queen Esthers and Hamans filling the place with screeching rattles. There was a pirate and her damsel in distress. An ugly duckling with the wings of a swan. Then Leo's green eyes were close to mine and I could smell the sweet taste of alcohol on his breath. A drink, I asked. Whisky, he said. On its way, I said Barman!

We talked a little. He said he didn't really have a regular job at the moment. He painted houses, he said. Did a bit of this and that. We danced together, his hands on my skin, his rough palms moving up my back and folding over my shoulders. Let's go now, he said. But I know the guy who's giving the party, I said; I haven't been here long enough. I know what, he said, tell him you have a headache and I'm taking you home in my car.

I walk away from the window. Fixing my hard-on in my underpants. I could spit on the sidewalk if I wanted to. I could swagger. I could start a fight. I could transform into something that scares me. But I keep walking. Floating almost. I have a picture in my mind and I'm taking it to Olga. I smile at the memory of how Leo and I met. There have been others like him. So I know it won't last forever. But I know that when it passes, the memory of it will remain. The feeling, that is. And that in itself is enough.

NINE LIVES

We've just cleared the dishes away in silence, and I say: "I think I'll have dessert later." Because I don't think I can stand one more second at the table with you.

We move over to the living room, where the light is brighter; it's easier to read in here. Easier than in the bedroom, say. So I stretch out on the sofa, get back to my book. The ceiling-fan you installed last summer whirs around lazily; its constant background hum making it easier to focus on the page. And then, and then you say: "What?" From your armchair across the carpet. You say that, and expect me to come up with an answer. You're playing with the cat you brought home three weeks ago. That white, hairy, deaf Persian cat with the tail like a pendulum.

"What did you say?"

"Is everything okay?"

"Oh, yes, fine," I say. "I'm just trying to get through this story."

And carry on reading. I've been ploughing through this book for God knows how long. Still ten more stories to go, though with the way things are going, I'll never finish them all. That's the problem when you can't keep your mind on one thing — when you're distracted, when you're doing a million things at once — there's never an end in sight.

You're staring at me from the other end of the carpet as the cat settles down on your lap. And you start doing that thing with your leg, jiggling it up and down. I know exactly what you're trying to tell me: Let's go, let's get a move on. And I'll look over at you and say: You know, that's really irritating, that thing you're doing with your leg. Please stop. And you'll make one of those faces of yours, and I'll say: It's not as if I'm asking for much, am I?

The cat's fast asleep by now — or just pretending — its bum against your stomach, its tail hanging straight down, its head on your knee, unfased by that bouncing leg of yours. The stupid cat probably finds it reassuring.

"Is everything okay?" you ask.

"Yes, fine," I say. "I told you, everything's fine."

"Fine?"

"Fine."

I wish I could just say: You know, why don't you get out. Just go. Just give me some room.

"Let's do something," you say.

"Like what?"

"I don't know," you say. "Anything."

"I just want to finish this story," I tell you. "I'd rather just stay in here and finish the story."

Insist, and I'll change my mind. Tell me we have to go to a movie. That we have to go to a movie or for a walk. Right now. Tell me you've made plans to meet so-and-so for dinner and there's no way we can cancel at the last minute.

It's so fucking hot in here I can hardly breathe. The sweat tickles the underside of the skin on my forehead. Maybe I can keep it from pouring out, somehow, mind over matter. But you can't fool sweat, you know. You can't tell the body what to do. The body has a life of its own. There goes the cat, slinking down onto the floor, giving me one of its looks, then climbing back onto your lap.

"Did you see that?" you say.

"See what?"

"The cat."

"What about the cat?" I say.

"I think I'm going to go for a walk," you say.

So you get up, put the cat onto your chair, and walk to the door. The cat looks at you, sulkingly; it's not at all pleased to have its cushion taken away.

"I'm taking a key," you say.

Then take it and go.

The door shuts behind you like a punch in the stomach, and then silence. This is better. Peace and quiet at last. Things can be so still when there's no-one in your field of vision. If only it wasn't so stifling in here. And sticky. Time to invest in an air-conditioner; that's the next item on the list. But first you'd better find a new job, a proper nine-to-five job this time, one that'll pay for more than just our day-to-day existence. The sweat comes off my forehead into the palm of my hand and I massage my neck and bring my fingers down to my chest, the hairs brittle with dampness. Everything's so moist and humid. When I get up there'll be an oval sweat-stain on the sofa. All summers are the same here; there's no relief from this constant heat.

Good idea. Iced coffee. Treat yourself for once. Relax more. Use this time to gather your thoughts. Come on cat, let's have some iced coffee. Let's walk from the living room to the kitchen, a lovely walk, stretch our bones. If I went out looking, I know where I'd find you. I know where I would go on a night like this.

The last time I followed you there we were like strangers. I watched the boy cruise you amongst the trees, watched how you kept his interest by ignoring him, walking from the bushes to the statue of the seagull overlooking the beach. I felt left out and I felt responsible, as if I was to blame for what was happening to us. As if it was up to me to put a stop to this and get things back on track. As if I should be taking your hand and leading you home.

I fill the kettle and wait for the faint hiss. I pour some of the water back into the sink. There's no air in this kitchen. The smell sticks to the walls and snakes its way into the cupboards. I must get a lid for this rubbish-bin. A garlicky smell wafts up from the dishes in the sink. And there won't be any clean teaspoons. I just know it. The milk in the fridge will be sour. And it's been two weeks, maybe more, since we last went to the supermarket. We should paint the kitchen walls again. The grease around the cooker needs to be wiped, and the spot where the rain came in last winter has turned to mould. Sweat and soap fumes rise up from my chest. Please, not another summer of this. Not another whole fucking summer to get through.

Just abandon yourself. That's what you said. We were standing right here in the kitchen on the night I brought you back from the new gay bar on Ibn Gvirol Street, and you said: Just abandon yourself to the heat. Give in.

You wore that white vest of yours, damp with sweat-marks under your armpits. I'd watched you earlier that night in the bar, laughing at everyone's jokes; how they all wanted to impress you and fill your silences with their offerings. You stayed behind after your friends had left and waited for me to come over. You thought I'd want to impress you, too. But you were the one who was impressed. You told me you were. What a handsome man, you said. Your eyes are so... so...

I made iced coffee for us when we got home. You said: Not too much milk; it makes my throat go all phlegmy. Then you came and hugged me from behind, the humidity making my back stick to you. We must have been naked by then. So quick to dive into intimacy, like undernourished children. And I wanted to say: That feels perfect; let me put my head into the hollow of your neck. I wanted to lick the beads of sweat off your upper lip, so I watched all evening to see if you'd wipe them away. But you never did. You didn't seem to notice.

The water clicks off.

I don't care anymore. Come on, cat, let's go back to the living room.

We went to the beach then. An apartment right by the sea, you said, you lucky bastard. And we laughed, like conspirators. Just look how those first few days keep coming back to me like possibilities for a new beginning. You were kind and gentle that morning when you stayed for breakfast. Pass the butter, please. And the jam, please. Come on, stop looking at me like that, you said. Please don't. I'm the one who should be staring, you said. I can't believe how lucky I am.

We spent the day together. I lent you an old pair of swimming shorts. You said: Maybe I should go home and get my own. But these look fine on you, I said. It's a pity to miss the sun. Now's the best time to catch a tan. And we walked down Sderot Nordau, holding hands as we crossed the Park and took the stairs down to the Hilton Beach. We spread our towels out on the hard sand near the water. I lay on my back and closed my eyes, imagining we were alone, no-one there but us. And then I must have laughed, I know I did, because you asked me what was so funny, and I might have said I was just being paranoid. Or perhaps I touched your shoulder and you said: Ah, that smile of yours. It's... it's...

There goes your cat. Crawling off the armchair and gliding towards the living room door. It turns to look at me and then waits for you to come in. It can sense your keys in the door, but I can hear them wrestling with the lock. Then you open the door and I see how dark it is behind you.

"Nice outside?"

"Very," you say. "I went for a swim."

"A swim? Out there in the dark?"

"It was nice," you say. "I was the only one."

You're framed in the doorway now, your hands in your

pockets. You're a beautiful man. A beautiful, beautiful man. The cat comes to sit beside me and keeps its eyes on you. Come and pick it up. Can't you see it wants to rest on your lap.

"I brought you some chocolate," you say.

"I'll have it in the morning," I say.

"Are you coming to bed?"

"Soon," I say. "I'll be there soon."

You stand there deliberating whether to come in. Should I. Should I not. And I imagine bright yellow daisy petals tossed about the room. I push the cat off the sofa and go back to my book. You know I'm in the middle of this story.

"Still on the same one?" you say.

I try not to hear you leave the room, shower, piss, turn off the light in the bathroom, in the bedroom, by the bedside. And sleep.

Just wait now. Slow down. Let him sleep. Then it's quiet again. How come everything becomes contaminated so quickly? Every sound spreading everywhere and into everything. There's no point in trying to finish the story if I can't focus. Best just to go to bed. Take a shower and get into bed. So I walk to the bathroom, my eyes fixed ahead, not wanting to see whether you're asleep or just pretending. Past our bedroom, the spare room, empty, as if anyone would want to visit this house.

I let the hot water massage the back of my neck, soften my muscles. I can forget the heat out there for a while. I used to like sitting here on the shower floor, watching you on the toilet, trying to turn you on. I can't imagine touching your body now. Just the thought of your sour smell makes me want to be sick. As if all these years of knowing you have made you uglier to me, as if familiarity really does breed contempt. I wash the soap off my skin and stand in front of the mirror, trying to see myself, but all there is is the shape of a body, as if someone is walking towards me through a fog. I towel myself down; pointless really, as I'll only start sweating right away. I hang the towel up and walk to our bed.

The covers are on the floor and you're lying on your back. Your cock semi-hard with sleep. I touch your side, accidentally, with my elbow, and whisper: I'm sorry. You mumble something, only pretending to have been woken. I lie on my stomach, facing you, and you let me look at you as much as I want to, as much as I need to. How can you feel so safe in here? How can you just lie there and know that no harm will come to you? I have to get away from this bed.

"Where to?" you ask.

"It's just too fucking hot in here."

"It's late," you say.

"I know. But I'm hungry."

"Have some chocolate."

"Okay," I say. "I will."

"Good night then," you say.

I don't switch the light on in the kitchen. I boil the water and feel around in the cupboard for the coffee and the sugar. I take a mug down from the shelf. There aren't any clean teaspoons, not one fucking teaspoon, and I'm not about to go digging around in the sink. I use my fingers to put what feels like two teaspoons of coffee and two sugars into the mug. I lick the sugar off my fingers and a grain of coffee sticks to my tongue. The light in the fridge isn't working, and the bloody milk is off. Best get back to the story, then so I can say: I did it; I started the story and I finished it and now I can go on. But your snoring follows me. Like dripping water. Please. Stop. Please please please just stop. Why can't everything just shut the fuck up?

"Sweetheart," you call.

What.

"Come to bed."

Don't. Please don't.

I'll just sleep here on the couch like I used to. You know how I used to hate having strange men in my bed. But I was always too.. too.. what? polite? afraid? to tell them to leave. They'd sleep in my bed and mess up my sheets and leave their sweat and after-shave on my mattress, and then I'd have to throw everything in the wash and start all over again. But now you're in the bed and the couch has been taken over by the cat, its eyes tightly shut as it stretches out.

Just a few more lines, then the last line, and that's it. The story's over. Finished. Just that much closer to getting through the whole book. On the way back to bed I remember the night Peter came to stay. It was another of these unbearable summers and we couldn't get to sleep. The only way to bring an end to the day was to fuck, so we did, and I thought: At least now the day doesn't have to go on forever. So now, when I get back to bed, back to you, and there's no choice but to sleep, you turn to me.

"What's the matter?" you say.

"What?"

"We can talk if you like."

"No, no. Just sleep."

"Are you sure?" you say.

"Yes, I'm sure," I say, lying on my back, my hands at my sides.

"Sleep well," you say.

Go. Please. Just go.

"Are you okay?" you say, your hand on the dampness on my stomach.

Please don't touch me.

"I'm fine," I say.

"Get some sleep," you say. "Try and get some sleep."

It must be almost morning by now. The air's a little

78

cooler, and it's so quiet out there, just the occasional car on Yehuda Maccabi Street heading for work, or a taxi bringing someone home, and the birds waking in the trees outside the Music Conservatory at the end of the road. I stroke your back and curl up at your side. A memory comes to me: a mustard-coloured carpet and my mother on the floor beside my bed. She would read to me every night, and sometimes she'd finish the story before I'd fallen asleep, and she'd say: Can I go now? And I'd say: Yes, yes, you can go now.

PERMANENT DISTRACTION

So this is what they call pitch dark. Even with my eyes open I can't see a thing. Two nights ago when the bombing started, they stopped all calls to my mother; it upsets her, they said when I ring the hospital. I'd asked the duty nurse to let my mother know we were fine, even though I knew she'd prefer not to know. My mother does not like to know. Just as she wouldn't let me tell her where my father was when he called for the first time after he'd left us and moved in with his new wife. I'd just finished my high school exams and had a month left before going into the army. I remember how excited everyone else was about joining, eager to do what their fathers and brothers had done before them.

From that I will protect my son.

I want to hear my father's voice again, quiet and uncertain, the way people talk when they cloak their feelings in pensiveness, when they take time to think before they speak. My father had learnt to do that through shell-shock and through leaving this place. And now, sitting here on the armchair *Sabba* George brought when he came to live with us, I think about him, and about that; about taking time. I hug it to my chest like a bird, make it stop and be still, allow itself to be held. I have a son now. A son who doesn't know what'll be expected of him. I have a son, and there's no getting away from that. I will never again have the luxury of being just me. There will always be something — someone — between me and the world.

Three days into the war and still no word from my father, not even to say he got the message I left about the death of his mother. Not even to ask how Daniel was. Not even to suggest we pack our stuff and get away from this war, like Miri's mother had done from London. She'd said:

Close the café, take Daniel out of school, leave the house, and get on the next plane to Heathrow.

"He's too selfish to think about anyone," Miri had said.

"He does care," I said, sitting down to sip cold coffee, showing her that no matter what, I would stay.

"Oh, Benjamin," she said.

"What 'Oh, Benjamin'?"

She was hanging washing on the clothes rack in the kitchen. Miri spoke as if she was stating the obvious, as if only an idiot would argue with her. And because of that it was all spite, all venom, and all fear. She knew that confusion silenced me, that doubt stopped me from putting up a fight, and that's why she didn't trust my silences. I had to get away from her, from the mistrust that seemed to be festering now.

"He just cares about himself," she said.

She took the last T-shirt from the washing machine and draped it over the rack.

"It's not easy for him," I said.

"Nothing's easy," she said, turning to the freezer for a chicken for Friday, caught up in her own drama.

"He'll call," I said.

I left the room and took Daniel downstairs to play football on the lawn.

"Why's mommy angry?" he said.

"She's just a little worried, Dan-Dan," I said.

"Are *you* worried?" he said.

"We'll both look after you," I said. "And *Sabba* George."

There'd been time to bury my grandmother before the bombing began. It had been a cold and rainy afternoon in the new cemetery just outside Tel Aviv, and we'd all been anxious to get home. Standing in the mud by her grave, our gas masks in plastic bags beside us, I knew we'd have to postpone our mourning. The last nine months we'd spent waiting for the cancer to finish eating away at her lungs had been a kind of grieving. Now there was only one thought: Will we make it back home before the war starts? So while Iraqi missile launchers took aim, and the world's warships got ready to fire back, *Sabba* George removed his coat and covered the shroud around *Savta* Anna's tiny body, insisting they bury her with it.

Daniel's glee was unbounded. When I play with him I am four years old again, grateful to have a friend who wants to include me in his games. I want to keep him to myself, to protect him and to raise him to always feel comfortable in the choices he makes. Do I believe that Miri can give him that? What will she do when it's time for him to go to war? For it's the women in this country, more than the men, who expect their sons to go and fight. To her, I am a coward. I should go to her now, leave the darkness of the living room, walk down the passage to where she is lying in bed, reading the kind of books she says are good for wars and long journeys, and say to her: I will never be my father.

She almost met him once, and has mistrusted him since then. We were in London for our wedding; Miri wanted to be close to her parents, and my father was in Paris with his new wife. My mother was in hospital, her first of what has turned out to be seven years. Miri and I had moved into a squat near King's Cross, just off Gray's Inn Road. We were happiest then. We'd found the place with three students we'd met at the youth hostel on Euston Road. A German called Oliver, and a gay couple from Glasgow, Myles and Rajib. Miri was convinced they were fucking the German while we were out.

A week after we found the squat I called Paris from a call box. My father's new wife spoke as if we knew each other, and the rain came through the broken windows. She got me to tell her things about myself, and about Miri, and my mother. She said all her children were married, she had grandchildren who called my father grandpa. She made me give her the number of the call-box; she would pass it on to my father and get him to call me that evening. She'd make sure he did. I said I'd wait for his call at eight. She said it was also raining in Paris.

Now the rain is a comfort, its reassuring patter on the drain pipes when you're warm inside. Living in this country, winter is like a foreign land, so different to the perpetual heat of the extended summers. They're saying that if the missiles have chemical warheads the rain will wash everything into the earth. Then, five years ago, in London for the wedding, I walked back to the squat and I was drowning. The void that opens up with the death of a parent was becoming bigger, big enough to engulf me. When I got back to the flat I asked Miri to hold me, and we lay on the carpet, our arms around each other, the warmth of our stomachs pressing together. Oliver was naked on his mattress, plucking out pubic hairs with Miri's tweezers, then piling them up in a copper ashtray by his bed. The curves of his body soft and hairless; the folds of flesh under his nipples making him look like an overgrown baby. His cock rested on the sheet between his legs. And I thought: What would it be like to crawl across the floor and lick the inside of his foreskin, to taste a thing I had not tasted before?

"I hate Indian food," Oliver said. "It stinks."

Myles and Rajib were making a curry stew on the gas burner they'd stolen from a camping store in Covent Garden.

"Did you hear me?" Oliver said, "I said I hate Indian food."

"I heard you," Rajib said. "And I love you."

"Do you know what my father says about Indian food?"

Rajib smiled as he grated fresh cucumber into a bowl, then stirred in some yoghurt and coriander and garam masala.

"Hey," Oliver said. "I hate Indians, as well."

He put the tweezers down and reached under his pillow for the plastic sachet of marijuana. He sprinkled some onto a Rizla with tobacco, and rolled himself a joint. Then he stuffed the packet back under his pillow and smoked alone, carefully burning his pubic hairs in the ashtray with the tip of his cigarette. That's what we should have organised for the war: marijuana, cheap wine and some hippie friends.

Sabba's leather chair, the armchair that is a memory from childhood, is too yielding, too comfortable — the padding softened, the leather worn away — and I don't want to go to sleep. Or is it that I don't want to be woken? To fall asleep, now with the bombs coming every night, is to let go of consciousness knowing that you're going to be shocked back into fear and panic and a certainty that you're going to die right there and then.

At the window, drawing open the curtains, expecting an entire audience to be on the other side, I watch our neighbour walking his fox terrier in the rain and dark. His wife and daughters have gone to stay on his parents' kibbutz in the South. They and I had been on the same number 5 bus yesterday before the evening "curfew." I got off on the corner of Nordau and Dizengoff Streets to walk down to the beach; they carried on to the Central Bus Station, where he'd see them off.

The sea had been rough, the air cold and salty. A windsurfer out beyond the marina — his sails red and green and white — was riding up against the waves to do somersaults with his board. I sat on the rocks by the water's edge; the beach and the promenade behind me deserted.

I'd come down here with *Sabba* George that first summer in the army, when my mother had gone into hospital, and my father had been away for a year already, and *Sabba* had called me his son, had said that when he dies, I will be the one to say *kaddish*.

Yesterday, the sea spray had been cold, and I was restless; I got up to walk along the beach. The windsurfer was bringing his board back to shore right in front of me. I noticed his shirt and towel and could see the outline of the box with his gas mask under his T-shirt. He unscrewed the sail and dragged both sail and board onto the sand.

"Not many people out here," he said.

"Everyone's getting ready for tonight," I said.

"No gas mask?" he said.

"I live nearby," I said.

"I like coming here," he said. "I feel safer out in the open. I saw the bombs fall last night."

His eyes were bright green and his body smelt of washing powder and the rubber of his wet-suit; the taste of anticipation in my mouth, as he peeled his wet-suit off and left it on the sand beside him. The muscles on his chest were more defined from the effort of holding onto the sail, and the green veins along the insides of his arms stood out like wiring, like a map, an undercurrent to draw me in.

"Do you want to come for a swim?" he said.

He pulled off his shorts and stood looking at the water. His back was covered in goose-bumps, and smooth, except for the soft patch of light-brown hair growing at the base of his spine. He turned then, his cock almost hard, his pubic hair dense, to say: "The water's not that cold, you know."

"I need to get home," I said. "My wife'll be worried."

"Your wife?" he said.

He folded his arms across his chest and let my eyes wonder over his body.

"So, you're married," he said. "Any kids?"

"One," I said.

He smiled the way I have seen other men smile when they know they are about to seduce a man who belongs to someone else.

"Daniel," I said. "His name's Daniel."

"I'm Nadav," he said.

We didn't shake hands and he didn't wait to hear my name. He picked up his wet-suit and carried it into the sea, left it floating in the shallow waters, and dived away from the shore. He didn't swim far, and while he swam I stood, not wanting to move, only to watch, to be this close to saying yes, and to still go home untouched, my skin intact, worthy of holding my son against it. And there is also a familiar feeling of guilt, as if I'd used Daniel's existence to entice and reject this man. Then he came back, fished his wet-suit out of the water, rinsed the sand off it, and walked up to where I was standing, his cock much smaller now. He dried himself off and wrapped the towel around his waist and we stood together and watched the tip of the sun touch the edge of the horizon which seemed to rise up, just a fraction, to meet it.

Getting married was supposed to kill off these desires, but now, with death so close and unavoidable, all I want is another man next to me. Back in London then, I remember how cold it was outside, the biting chill that comes after a London rain in winter. I stood inside the telephone booth, hugging myself in a thick army coat. When my father hadn't called by eight-thirty I dialled his number in Paris. The voice on the answering machine was his, asking for messages, saying he'd call back as soon as possible. I watched a Japanese dancer in the forecourt of King's Cross Station, her face white with make up, her fingers stiff. The music crackled from small speakers as I moved

87

towards the people that had gathered around her. And then as if out of nowhere, someone ran past me, parted the crowd, and grabbed her cap of money, and without missing a beat, she lifted her kimono to her hips and ran after him, shouting: "Come back, you fucker. Give me that or I'll fucking kill you."

Back at the flat we smoked Oliver's marijuana while he slept. I told Miri that my father wasn't feeling well, that they'd decided to go back to the States the next morning. I lay on my back, my hands behind my head, Miri's cheek on my stomach. She slipped her tongue between the buttons on my shirt and licked patterns on my skin, her tongue damp and warm. I wanted to warn her, to tell her that this would be the first time I would lie to her, and if she let me, I'd keep going.

The next morning when she went walking with Myles and Rajib to Regent's Park, I asked Oliver to fuck me. I stood facing the wall, my hands on the greasy wallpaper, while he held onto my arse and shoved his cock in and out of me until we came.

How well do I know this house? The passage going through to the bedrooms, the walls with Miri's tapestries, fabric and embroidery and gold brocade, collages inspired by Hundertwasser. Daniel's nursery school drawings: stick figures and a bright yellow sun, an imperfect circle surrounded by hyphens. The dining room where we sat the first night of the *shiva*, after dinner, Miri, *Sabba* George, Daniel and I, staring at the radio and listening for passwords, the dreaded words used for emergency call-ups. *Sabba* George wondering what more could be lost. Daniel hoping they'd choose his daddy. Miri got up to do the dishes, and all I could think was: Please don't say those two words. And then I stopped listening. I knew then that I wouldn't go even if they did call me up. It was up to me to free myself.

I went to Miri in the kitchen, leaving *Sabba* George and Daniel in the dining room with the box of chocolates her mother had sent us from London. Miri was at the kitchen table with her head in her hands. That's when London started coming back to me. A time in our lives when nothing was known, when nothing, no definite clues could point to this present. No indication as to where we would land up. Miri's shoulders were tense under my fingers, as if her flesh had hardened, not into muscle, but stone, or sediment. And I wanted to say: Remember our squat, the curry and rice and marijuana? Remember walking along the river all the way to Richmond? It's only been five years since then. How difficult could it be to go back? At least there nothing changes.

I knew that if I didn't move away I'd land up telling her everything. So I filled the sink with hot water, squirted in washing-up liquid, and let my hands be scorched. I thought about my mother in hospital, about what they were doing to her. How easy it is to abandon our parents. How quickly we forget the bodies we no longer touch. And as if to make sure I remembered, Daniel's shrill laughter shot into the kitchen. *Sabba* George must have been teasing him; he had a way of teasing you that made you feel invited into some exclusive game, a club where laughter and silliness were valued. As a young boy I loved to sit in their kitchen, watching *Savta* Anna top-and-tail green beans, grate carrots, and *Sabba* George would put his elbow on the table, roll up his sleeve, bring his little finger to his lips and make as if pumping up his bicep. And no matter how hard I pressed down — both of them laughing, *Savta* Anna saying: *Sabba*, stop it — I could never get the air out of his muscle.

And then when the bombs fall I am thrown back to the war ten years ago in Lebanon: shooting and flares lighting up the skies, the bitter taste of dust in my mouth, the

89

smell of burnt meat. My gun pressing into me from under the thin foam mattress. Officers shouting at us to get to the foxholes. And even in the darkness I knew what the others in the tent were doing: Slipping into their uniforms and boots, strapping on ammunition belts, grabbing their guns and going out to fight. And my thinking was this: They wouldn't even notice that I'm not there. I will pretend to be asleep.

Daniel's scream.

I grab him from *Sabba* George's arms and we run for the sealed room, the bathroom with its windows covered in plastic sheeting and masking tape, the plug holes blocked by rags soaked in bleach, the bathtub padded with blankets and cushions for Daniel to sit in.

"It's okay, it's okay," Miri closes and seals the door behind us.

You're safe, my boy. His screams are like a birth cry, his voice like sharp knives. I hold him while Miri tries to fit on his gas mask.

"He doesn't want it," I say.

"I don't care what he wants," Miri says.

Daniel is choking inside his mask. He pulls it off and I cover his head with my jacket.

A whisper: "*Abba*."

It is dark and the walls are shadows. Daniel is here at the armchair with his torch.

"What, son?"

"I can't sleep."

He puts his torch on the table next to me and climbs up onto my lap, tucking his head into my shoulder. He lifts my arm and wraps it around him.

"Tell me a story" he says.

"It's late, Dan-Dan," I say. "Time for bed."

I pick him up, the weight of his head heavy on my shoulder.

"Hold the torch," I say. "Hold the torch so we can see where we're going."

We climb the stairs and I tuck him into bed. I shine the torch onto the fluorescent stars stuck to his ceiling, feeding them with light before switching the torch off again. I sit by his bed as the darkness envelops us. It's a quiet darkness. A warm, comforting darkness with no shadows.

THE DEATH OF OTHERS

Tell them my father's story.

Saul's father, Nathan Ben-Ami, died in Ashkelon's Barzilai Hospital before the doctors could figure out why he was there. Not because it was a quick and painless death, but because he couldn't put his finger on the pain and say: Here, doctor, this is where it hurts. He was as quiet as he'd been for the past few months. And after they drew blood and pasted electrodes to his chest, the glue making brittle clumps in his chest hair, he walked back to his bed, head down, counting each step. And then, when they told him they couldn't find anything wrong, and maybe they should run a new series of tests, he nodded, and seconds later breathed his last breath.

It was summer then; the air inside the hospital was humid and stagnant, all the fans had been hogged by the receptionists. Nurses sprinkled talcum powder onto their finger tips before picking up a syringe. Doctors who couldn't postpone urgent surgery had two nurses each to pat sweat off their faces, necks and arms. Patients on the operating table, their flesh sliced open, sweated like pigs. It was a summer not unlike every other summer in Israel.

When he left he left without warning, just the farewell bow and he was gone. Betty thought of her mother. She thought of herself at nineteen saying goodbye to her mother. Saul came into the room as she stood at Nathan's bedside, both hands holding a glass, gulping down water like a child. She walked past him to ask the doctor if he could come and have a look. Then she told the nurse to please call this number, and went back to the room to wait for Marcelle , her sister.

What would she do with no-one to shelter her now from the world and from the hatred of her son?

She and Nathan would go everywhere together. He joined her on her weekly trips to the supermarket, waiting at the cheese counter to chat to David Bulgari, who'd found religion at about the same time Nathan had. The last time she came to pick up her sliced Emek and block of salty cheese, Nathan had said: You haven't forgotten the candles, have you? And she, who didn't need a list to shop, reached into the trolley for the blue box, its colour as it had been when she got here twenty years ago, and she showed him the braided candles. *Voila.*

From when he began taking long walks on the beach and preferred to spend time with his own silences, she joined him every now and again for *shacharit*, the prayers at dawn, at the new synagogue in Barnea. From the women's gallery she'd watch him swaying back and forth, keeping his eyes on the page, lifting them only to exchange a word or two with Haim Samson from Bombay, who since his son had been blown up in Lebanon, clung to the warmth of the Almighty and wrapped himself in it like a beggar. And then Nathan would tap Haim Samson's shoulder, mumble something, and turn the pages for him.

And in these small gestures Betty saw the Nathan it had taken her just a few days to fall in love with, not the person he and the world had turned him into; a hard man, as difficult and stubborn and uncompromising as a brick wall. She told this to Saul when he sat her down with the photo albums only days after his father had died. Saul had asked for his father's story. They paged through the photos and Betty pointed to the pictures of another man who could quote to her from Mao and Marx and Mandela. All Nathan could do was quote the jargon of the Revisionists which he'd been fed on at home before his parents sent him to finish his education on a kibbutz. Nathan had told

Betty his English wasn't very good, even though his parents were one of the first South Africans to make *aliyah*, and he had no intention of trying to improve it.

And my English, Saul told me, is from television and the memory of a foreign lover. My mother and father gave me nothing.

That's fine, she'd said, only recently arrived in Israel, only recently a woman, only recently having left her mother in Port Elizabeth and sailed around Africa with her sister and brother-in-law.

And to get away from her dead father and the young man who insisted on fighting for his country. It sounded right to her then. It did. But, she told Saul, Nathan didn't have the kind of passion she was familiar with. His ardour wasn't that of the idealist and the blind romantic willing to take on the world single-handed. It was — and forgive me for saying this — it was the hysteria of the self-loathing and the shat-upon, eager to transform himself into something his father could approve of. The father who sent him off to live on a kibbutz, saying they'd give him things he and his mother never could. So Nathan insisted they speak Hebrew and laughed at her mistakes and mispronunciations, and then he said: Come, let's go for a walk in the orange groves.

Okay, she said. I'd like that.

The sun was setting purple on the day, each orange basted with dim light. Nathan pointed out the white horse in the paddock, it's skin dotted with flies.

Saul insisted I was zigzagging between his father and his mother. He said: My father comes first; talk about him. He was the first to die. Tell his story.

Trust me, I said. It takes one story to tell another. Stories are made up of more than just themselves.

And so it was that Nathan left his wife Betty clinging to water. Perhaps he wanted to go on alone, or maybe he was kind enough to let her finish the things she'd never had the chance to do. Silly man, after bullying her into forgetting her past and relinquishing everything she loved, did he really think she would be able to do that.

And that monster son of hers was no help at all.

But the forgetting and relinquishing was a choice. It was too late to start saying goodbye. All she knew were ways to keep shutting herself off from everything she longed for. Like the friends from back home who over the years came to live here, bringing into the world children of their own, calling her every Passover to fill her in. To end each conversation she would make plans to meet up, but more often than not would cancel just days before. And what did she long for? If she was pressed for a word she would have said "love." But it was more than that. There was a daughter her body missed and a love that could have been hers to keep.

What's all this love she could have had? This love she missed out on.

I could give you examples, I said, but that would be giving away too much.

All that you'd be giving away, he said, is that you know fuck-all about love.

Every example I have is about a love that devours you. A love that pushes you to disfigurement and insanity. And if I'd known then, I would have said to him: Saul, look at you. Look what love is doing to you. Obsessed by someone you hardly know. Pouring your stories out like a bulemic. Anything to stop yourself from grieving. All this self-disclosure to conceal your sadness. Love is death, sweet Saul, not life. But I didn't say anything. And why not? I kept quiet because I knew the less I told him about himself the less he'd know about me. Instead, I told him about a man who went mad when they killed the boy he loved, and about the stories he made up about the boy's death, and about

96

him loving the lice his lover had left in his pubic hair.

Get back to my story now. I don't want you confusing it with the stories of others. And don't forget the one place Nathan refused to go with her.

Whenever Betty wanted to visit her sister, Marcelle, Nathan would drive her to the house on *moshav* Sde Moshe, then he'd drive home and wait in a way she'd never know. When he found religion towards the end of his life, Saul would watch him on their balcony overlooking the park praying in his shorts and sandals. On the days they spent apart, Saul would find excuses to stay away from home. He couldn't bear to be alone with either of them. They fought for his love in disgusting ways.

There wasn't room for others in Nathan's house, so he merged them into one. Betty and Saul became him, and whenever they were away he was unwhole. That's why when he saw his son leaving, Nathan gave himself up to speechlessness and made the silence part of him. He began to purge his mind of them all and fill it with the escape route called God.

At sundown, Nathan would drive back to the *moshav* and hoot three times. And the way back to their flat behind the Rachel Cinema in Afridar on not a word about Marcelle or Leon passed between them. Betty spoke about Saul's primary school and then about high school and then about him being a soldier. And Nathan nodded and kept all disagreements to himself. He said: That idiot Benny Marx still owes me money for all those appliances he took from the shop. I'm going to say something if he doesn't pay by the end of the month. And Betty would say: There's such wonderful fruit in the market this time of year. It's a shame not to buy more. And he'd say: So, why not buy some? And she, still waiting for a request, would say: What would I do with it all? It's just the two of us now. And he, if everything had been different and he hadn't been sliding further away, would have said: Make some jam. Please make some of that nice watermelon *confeyt*.

There was the night (not the only one) that Betty slept over at Marcelle and Leon's. Nathan had a vague idea why, and even though he never mentioned it, whenever he drove his wife to the *moshav* after that, he'd say: So I'll come and pick you up later, *beseder*? And she was always ready before he got there, saying goodbye to Marcelle, Leon, and their son, Simon, and apologising for Nathan's stubbornness. You know how he is, she says to her sister, who pulls a chair up beside her in the hospital and holds her hand. He's been preparing for this silence, Betty says.

Since Nathan began closing in on himself, as Saul called it, Betty had grown closer and closer to her sister and clung to this intimacy like a buoy. She nurtured it as one nurtures hope, and feared it as one fears having to admit that one is a child forever. And when her son went into the army she was faced with her husband's withdrawal and with her ever-growing and painful need for a place to rest and cry.

So she *did* things.

What a choc-a-bloc-full parcel I sent Saul, she'd tell Marcelle. I'm not sure what he likes anymore. Do you think it's okay to be sending him cigarettes? Don't tell Nathan, she'd say, and besides — straightening her dress and looking down into her lap — as it is, he sees nothing nowadays. Just him and his silent prayers. She leans closer to Marcelle, takes a cookie from the saucer and sits back in her chair. You know, she says, he sent Saul a Bible from the hospital. The boy mailed it back to him with a note that they'd given him one at the swearing in ceremony at the end of basic training. As if Nathan didn't know.

All this talk talk talk and scurrying after things to say, because Betty knew her sister insisted on piercing sores that had long since scarred over and disappeared. Marcelle would delve in and grind, and Betty would recoil and come back for more, share a little then clamp up. Marcelle would set the *koeksusters* down on the long trays, letting them soak up the syrup they'd been dipped in. Shining with sweetness, still warm from the oil. She would come back to the breakfast nook and sit with Betty. They'd drink their tea, green now from the handful of mint, and nibble from the saucer of *ma'amul* biscuits Marcelle's neighbour had brought her.

Marcelle says: Remember Lorenzo's coffee-house just by Main Street, near the campanile, with those wicker stools. The smell of black coffee still reminds me of that place. We used to go there every Saturday after the bioscope.

I hardly remember, Betty says. I hardly remember anything. Who can remember things from such a long time ago.

Oh, honestly, *motek*, every week with Joe and Shirley and what's her name, the one who married an Afrikaner, and then ran off to live in Brussels. Don't you ever wonder what became of those people? I can't stop thinking about it all lately. Remember Johnnie and the fish-and-chip shop in Swartkops? Where's he now? Things happen to people we used to see every day and now we know nothing about them. *Niks*, hey. Remember that *moffie* with the high heels who worked at the Wimpy? Those silk scarfs of his and the way he walked. God, he was a sight to see.

How do you remember all these things? Betty asks.

What do you mean? How can you forget, is what I'd like to know.

Even when Betty sits next to Nathan in the car with the tray of *koeksusters* on her lap he wouldn't touch a thing, and wouldn't taste a morsel. But he can't stop from smelling his mother's kitchen, the one room in the house that survives in exile. The kitchen with the high stools at the marble surface. He'd sit there on the weekends he came home from the kibbutz and follow his mother's hands kneading the dough. But Nathan refuses to touch anything that comes out of that man's house. Betty stopped trying and gave up hoping, and the whole business between Nathan and her brother-in-law stopped being important.

They came to tell her he was a good man. He only knew how to do good for others. Since he started coming to the synagogue he's been a happy man. That's what they told her: a happy man. And there were those who knew he died because he wanted to, because he believed it was better not to live at all than to start from scratch and admit to too many things to talk about. They sat with Betty and spoke about their sons in the army, how proud they were of them. And they asked her why Saul never calls. Their sons keep asking how he's doing. All the time.

It's a good thing Nathan sold the business, Shoshana Menachem says to her. Who'd have run the thing now? Tell me, those people who bought the business, what do they know?

Betty let them talk. They filled the room with memories and commentaries, and gave her advice, thinking it would make things easier. You shouldn't have to... and wouldn't it be nice if you could... Only Haim Samson sat in silence on the mattress Marcelle had put out on the floor. He'd bought Betty a plate of rose-water delicacies rolled in coconut.

From Gita, he said. She sends her love.

Betty gathered up everything the mourners had scattered around the room and began to make space for herself. She drew the red velvet curtains that hid the walls. There's no point in going out, she said to Saul.

There was nothing for her to do out there. Inside, there was time to knit and cook, even if there wasn't anyone to knit and cook for. The steady clicking of the knitting needles was all the outside she needed. And whoever appeared in her body to say goodbye brought a group of others with them. Each guest with guests of their own. The chopping of parsley and coriander, the bubbling of pots and the spluttering of oil were her present. Only her son kept wanting more.

He'd come into the living room and stare. He'd stand before her as if he was on his knees. But she had nothing to give him. So she made him cream-and-garlic tongue, his favourite, which she'd stopped making while Nathan was on his way back to religion. Saul ate the tongue with mashed potatoes and soaked up the gravy with Friday's *challah*. Like his father. And, like his father, he was too scared to ask for anything that could be answered with a no. Like: Tell me what's going to happen when you're gone.

On nights like these, Saul wished for ten brothers and sisters, and a place to go that was home but not the house he grew up in.

The night she'd stayed at Marcelle's was the night Bernie Solomon came to live in Israel. Bernie had no family in this country, nor anywhere else in the world, so he came to Marcelle. Because of her mother. Even though Miriam Kaplan had gone on about Bernie Solomon doing nothing but harm to the State of Israel, him and that communist son of his, terrorists the lot of them. Marcelle had discussed it with Betty and Betty kept it from to Nathan. God knows why. It's not like she had anything to hide. But then, just because she kept the truth to herself didn't mean no-one else could see it.

Betty, Marcelle, and Leon went to fetch Bernie Solomon from the airport. Betty remembers the *hamsin*, because Bernie took his jacket off as soon as they left the terminal, then his waistcoat before they got into the car, then he loosened his tie and opened his top button. *Goed*, he said, that's better. So dry and dusty. Just like the bloody *berg* winds back home. It's winter there, you know. Jo'berg's cold and PE's wet. I visited your mom before I left.

Betty struggled and fought against what Bernie Solomon might say. She kicked out in every direction. Making sure they wouldn't have to walk past the other grave in that cemetery. And how's Peter, she wanted to say, a girl again of nineteen, ready to blush.

Leon, by then the head of the regional council of *moshavim* and an up-and-coming politician, told Bernie Solomon how lucky he was. He said things were changing in the country. It's not like it used to be. Not like when we first got here. You're lucky, he told Bernie. You're lucky to get here at a time like this. I mean... and his voice trailed off.

Betty's last letter from her mother. The one in which she told her that Peter had gone off to South West Africa to join SWAPO. Or was it the ANC? Or the bloody Cubans for all she knew. So to cut a long story short: he was killed. Her mother said Bernie had no-one left in South Africa. Or anywhere else in the world for that matter. And how is the little *baba'le* coming along? When is the due date? I'm so looking forward to it.

And the day came before it should have. It came and went and expected to be forgotten.

Dead son or no dead son, Bernie was lucky. Betty might have said something, driving past the airforce base, then the cotton fields near Ashdod, the orange groves on the way to the *moshav*, but she was too embarrassed for her brother-in-law. Betty was already too much a mother, feeling the feelings of others, forgetting how to read her own.

Peter and Betty spoke about the school they were going to build. They sat opposite each other at the café near the campanile. He wore his clean beige trousers and white shirt, top button open. His voice soft and deep, telling her things. His eyes like unpeeled almonds, and his long fingers never resting for a second, playing in the air, stroking his cup of tea, always cold by the time he drank it. He'd down it in one gulp, then carry on talking. And she'd talk and she'd listen, for everything about him was to love.

Bernie Solomon said: Your mother used to tell me how you'd run to sit on her lap when you were a little girl. All you wanted was to curl up on her lap and cry.

Yes, said Betty.

A very special woman, your mother.

And Betty had wanted to say: Yes, so was your son. Very special. For these were the words that flashed through her mind, out of instinctive politeness and a genuine longing, and then vanished. But she said other things.

It's a shame I never saw her before she died.

Yes, said Marcelle, sitting next to her on the back seat.

She used to wait for your letters, Bernie said. And when they came, every word was like a breath of life. It's good she doesn't have to see what's been happening to that country.

And if Betty had had the words, she would have said: Sometimes, when I'm sitting in the kitchen, a light breeze blows in through the windows like muslin cloth and tickles my hands and face, and then I want to turn to him and say: Peter, is that still you?

You were supposed to tell them my father's story, he said.
I did, I said.

103

A BORN KING OF SOMETHING

Where do you live?
At the time I was working in the adjutant's office on a base
near Ramleh, mailing out call-up papers to reservists during the day and working nights behind the bar at a place
called *Schnapps*. I had my own room in a hostel for soldiers just outside Tel Aviv. Towards the end of the first of
my three years in the army, I told the military shrink I
was scared the other soldiers would beat me up in the
showers when they found out I was gay, so she had me
transferred to a base closer to home, one where I wouldn't
have to stay overnight.

What do you have to offer our company?
I woke at 3am with Moshe's sharp little prick stabbing at
the walls of my arse. I pushed myself up onto all fours and
bit into my pillow. He came in my bum and then fell asleep
beside me. I lay awake until morning. I watched him sleep
on his back and wanted to put my head on his soft hairy
tummy. The following morning, over coffee made in a
saucepan with a heating element, Moshe told me he ran a
pub in Tel Aviv. In the evening I was learning to pour
draught beer with a fine head. I worked at *Schnapps* with
Moshe for the next sixteen months, seven nights a week.

What are your main skills and achievements?
I'd change out of my uniform in the small kitchen by the
bar, leaving the curtains open while I dressed to let Moshe
watch me from the counter while he spoke to his suppliers
on the phone. Then I'd check the oil in the deep fryer and
make sure each table had a glass ashtray and four
Carlsberg coasters. I'd prepare slices of cucumber and
tomato and a bowl of shredded lettuce, which I'd use to

decorate the toasted cheese platter we served with chips and Syrian olives. Students from the ballet academy above the pub would come to drink at the bar on their way home. When they were there I walked around as if my body had been shaped by a life-time's worth of pliés, hoping one of the men would discover me and take me home. After work we went back to Moshe's flat and I sat on him until he came inside me. With him on his back I could manoeuvre his cock so it didn't bash into the walls of my arse.

What are your hobbies and interests?
The adjutant — his name was Nimrod — used to attack me with a craft knife and pin me to the wall behind my desk, saying: "Beg. Come on, beg. Say you worship the ground I walk on." He was short and plump and recounted in detail how he'd shot a man in the back during the war in Lebanon. His girlfriend objected to him working with me. With a *homo*, that is. About three months after I met Moshe, I discovered that my body was covered in lice: pubes, chest and armpits. I was given special shampoo at the military clinic, but Nimrod made me sit in the office until it was time to go home. He said he'd give me a lift back to Tel Aviv. We stopped off at his girlfriend's on the way. We stayed in the car and she leaned on his window while they talked about their wedding. He told her I was crawling with crabs. Then he drove me to *Schnapps* and said I should stop letting Moshe fuck me like a whore. He said he'd give me some money to pay the rent at the hostel if that's why I was doing it. That night I got rid of the crabs after Moshe had gone to sleep.

Have you any physical disability?
Simon — my boyfriend and best friend at the time — said that everyone knew big cocks hurt less than small ones. Simon had a very big cock. I never told him about Moshe.

Simon was serving in a reconnaissance unit on the Northern border and came to spend weekends at the hostel. While I was at work Friday and Saturday nights he'd watch TV in the communal living room downstairs. One Friday afternoon Moshe knocked on the door while Simon and I were in bed. We chatted for a while and then Moshe said he had to be going. He asked me to walk him to his car. We went up onto the roof, though, and Moshe said he really needed to fuck me, so I bent over the sink where the tenants did their hand-washing and let him poke around inside me. That evening Simon told me he was going to work in the fisheries in Alaska after the army. I still had fourteen months to go. I have an average-sized cock.

Please give details of any serious illnesses, operations or accidents (with dates).

Jonathan Mendel has appeared in my dreams since we were in nursery school together. He is my one true love. When we were seven, his Irish setter, Sean, chased me across their terra cotta patio. I jumped onto the table and fell through its glass top; a triangular shard stuck in my arse-cheek. I said to his mother that I couldn't feel a thing and that I didn't need a doctor; couldn't I just stay and play and have the glass taken out later? His mother drove me to Emergency where they stitched me up, and then she took me home. Another time, we went on holiday to Cape St. Francis where Jonathan's sister chased me down the corridor with a pair of scissors. I ran into the leg of a chair that was lying on its side and had four stitches sewn into the top of my foot by an Afrikaans doctor in Humansdorp. I insisted on sitting up and watching the doctor inject me around the wound and then stitch up my flesh. I wasn't allowed onto the beach for the rest of the holiday. That scar — now in the shape of a boomerang — has faded. I need a mirror to see the other scar.

Do you speak any foreign languages?
I was fourteen when my parents took me to Israel from South Africa. When I was first learning Hebrew I'd get confused, and Afrikaans words would slip out like memories. Once I woke up next to Moshe and spoke to him in English. He looked at me and said: "Do you realise what language you're speaking?" So I apologised, and translated what I'd just said into Hebrew. He barked back that he'd understood perfectly well what I'd said in the first place.

How do you get on with people?
I'd hoped to meet Moshe's flatmate. She was one of the only transsexuals in Tel Aviv. Moshe said she was the only one who wasn't a prostitute. She was a florist in a shop in the mall on Dizengoff Street. I wondered if Moshe had told her about me, and whether it would be a nice idea to pop in and introduce myself next time I passed by the flower shop.

How do you cope with pressure?
I learnt to love gin gimlets while working at *Schnapps*. I found the recipe in a book for bartenders under the counter. The book said they were popular amongst the colonials in Africa. I'd have my first one at ten, two hours before closing time. Moshe never let on if he knew I was drinking. I think the lime cordial took away the smell of the gin, just like fresh lemon juice washes any trace of garlic off your fingers. By the time we got home I was so drunk I'd sail up and down on him with my eyes closed until he grunted and came inside me. Sometimes I'd fall asleep before it was over and Moshe would have to catch me and lower me onto the bed so he could fuck me on my side. In the mornings I'd shower, put on my uniform, and take the bus to the base. My officer loved fresh croissants and, being on good terms with the cook, would smuggle a

pot of cardamom coffee into the office each morning. We'd dip the croissants into our army-issued sky-blue plastic cups of coffee and make loud eating noises and laugh and Nimrod would wave his craft knife at me and say: "When the fuck are you going to start working?"

What do you hope to get out of the job?
Simon came back from Alaska after the first fishing season. He said he was cold and homesick. I had a month to go before my army duty was over. I'd stopped seeing Moshe by then and had got a job in the kitchen at Senõr Sandwich, a sandwich bar on Ibn Gvirol Street. Simon introduced me to other gay men. Once we had an orgy and Simon said I was embarrassing him by asking everyone to fuck me.

Where would you like to be in five years time?
What?

Do you have any questions?
I don't remember what happened to Moshe or why I stopped working at *Schnapps*. I stuck it out .at Senõr Sandwich for a couple of months. I used to bring left-over sandwiches back to the hostel, having returned the slices of ham and cheese to the fridge, and I'd share them with the Russian immigrant couple in the next room. At some point, I started sleeping with the husband, but then they got offered a flat in Haifa, so I helped them pack and move. Simon and I drifted apart and recently I discovered he was having an affair with an ex of mine. He was always spiteful and resentful and never forgave me for leaving me. If I get this job I'm going to save up and go abroad for a while. Maybe for a couple of years. London perhaps. A friend of mine tells me that it's easy to find a job there if you're not picky about the kind of work you do.

109

PROFESSOR AND MRS PAINTER

They usually sit here if the table isn't taken, and at this time of day in the middle of the week Chez Laurent is always empty. He likes it that way, and she's just happy to get out. They've come from different ends of New York. The waiter brings them coffee in white mugs and a slice of chocolate cake with a knife; he knows them well and smiles when they ask for iced water. It's the heat, and he too resents it for what it forces him to acknowledge. The body, for one, and poverty. She halves the wedge of cake, lifts the triangular bit onto a paper napkin, and slides the other half towards her son, Hugo, the college professor.

Hugo lectures in anthropology at a community college in Brooklyn. He's an expert on hunting-arrows and Amazonian tribes; now he teaches "Introduction to American Anthropology." This is the job he found when he came back from the West Coast four years ago, just after Eric died. Now he's in New York watching his mother eat slowly, waiting for her to pass judgement, listening to her tell him that Ada Blumberg's cancer is back, that her children never visit, that the poor woman has to take taxis to and from the hospital. Every morning she hears her being sick upstairs, vomiting just above her head every time she goes to the bathroom.

"And you know about me and the bathroom in the morning."

"Have you been up to see her?" Hugo says.

"This is still the best chocolate cake," his mother says.

She wonders if this is the right time to tell him. She remembers the evening he told them he was gay, the way he'd used the news item on the television to say to them: What if that was me? She could use Ada Blumberg to talk about the lump they'd found. What an ugly word: Lump.

So fat and ugly.

"How does she look?"

"She looks like hell," his mother says. "What else could she look like?" as she sucks the foam off her cappuccino.

Hugo thinks about a mouse pulling its legs from a glue trap.

That morning he'd been grading assignments in the kitchen, the fan on low, the muslin drapes dulling the sunlight, the rubber plant by the kitchen window freshly watered, and she'd called to ask him out. She knew he didn't teach on a Thursday. She said: I'm going mad in this building. I need air. The air-conditioner's not working and I need to get out of here. Everyone I know is either sick or dead. Take me for coffee, Hugo. As if he should rescue her, lift her off the floor. As if he was the only man in her life.

Her demands excited him.

"What else is happening in the building?" Hugo says, pouring water from the jug, blocking the ice cubes from plopping out with his fingers.

"Nothing happens there," she says. "It's always the same. Not like yours."

So he tells his mother about the people in his building. New men are always moving in; he must be the oldest one there. She listens, and her eyes wander to the women two tables away, eventhough she's half blind without her glasses. Her son tells her about the youngster who sits on the steps out front with his skateboard. Everyone has to climb over the boy to get in and out of the building. What he doesn't say is this: The young man's skin glistens with sweat, and at noon when I am leaving the building I think about kneeling on the stairs to lick it off his back. He doesn't say that the boy's sunny greetings torment him, and that his own relentless desire fills him with disgust.

If these women have children, she thinks, they're either bankers or running their dead father's business.

Those trinkets and ornaments they're wearing; why do women make themselves look so ugly? She's always hated jewellery and make up; that kind of thing, she believes, is fine for the young and beautiful, or the ones way beyond hope. Her son had pierced his ear when he turned thirty. This constant frowning of his makes her want to cry, and his eyes that dart all over the place. I gave birth to this man, she thinks.

"Are you getting out much?" she says.

"Of course I'm getting out," he says. "I teach almost every day."

"What were you planning to do today?" she says, pulling her chair closer.

"It's too hot for plans," he says. "I've got papers to grade."

"We used to drive out to the ocean when you were little," she says.

"I remember," he says. "I don't like swimming."

"Of course you like swimming," she says. "You love Greece."

"Well, that's Greece," he says.

"You used to love swimming," she says. "You and your father."

The iced water runs through him like menthol. What with that and the air conditioning, the sweat will soon dry on his skin. Thank God there are no men to see the blotches that have spread out like ink stains under his armpits. The walk along St Marks to the subway had been torture; the journey cramped; his body a constant disappointment. And bare flesh so close to him on the subway. Hugo can't help touching other men, walking down the carriage, brushing against forearms and shoulders. He's a menace to himself and to others.

"Now I remember," his mother says. "You gave me your book here."

Hence the straw hat on the chair next to her, he thinks. The hat she hadn't worn in the ten years since he bought it for her in Peru, for if she had, she would have made sure he knew about it. She makes the memory sound like a happy one. As if her words were compliments. It's inappropriate for mothers to praise their sons. He could tell her about the tribe that forbids mothers to make eye contact with their sons; all communication is done through mediators.

"Here?" he says.

"Not at this table, no," she says. "But in this restaurant you did."

His coffee is luke warm and he drinks it in loud gulps. His shirt isn't sticking to his back and he stretches his legs out to the wall, careful not to touch her feet, his mother's new open-toed sandals. She's going to talk about his book. He likes it when she remembers things about him. Fifteen years since *Silent Hunters* came out, three years of living amongst Amazonian tribes and a book the *TLS* had called exciting. Praise from England — his mother's place of birth — always meant more to him.

"How long ago was it?" she says.

"Years," he says.

"It was a good book," she says.

"Was it?" he says.

He sits up and leans forward and two young men in vests walk in. Their bronzed skin is soft against tight cotton fabric. No sweat, just a glow, a sheen, a film that'll dry to velvet. One of them has a tattoo on his shoulder that looks like a swallow; the other has a pierced nipple that's pressing against the fabric of his vest. It makes Hugo feel fat. He sips his coffee and eyes his mother flattening cake crumbs onto her fingertips, as if she were killing ants. The men sit opposite each other between the art deco mirror and the poster of Ingrid Bergman in *Joan of Arc*.

The man facing Hugo opens his gym bag and takes out a book and notepad. The muscles in his shoulder sway with every movement. He runs a hand through his thick hair, still wet from the showers, and dries his palm on his jeans. He surveys the room while his boyfriend browses through the menu. Then, because he thinks no-one can see him, he glides a hand under his armpit and wipes the sweat off onto his thigh. I bet they ask for fruit juice, Hugo thinks; something to stir their protein powder into. His mother pinches the crumbs off her fingers with a napkin, then wipes the grease from the table.

"We've been coming here for years," she says.

"Do you still come here on your own?" Hugo says.

"Why would I do that?" she says.

"With Mrs Beilin," he says. "You used to come here with Heda Beilin."

"What made you think of her?" his mother says. "She's dead."

"Is she?" he says. "Her son's just published his third novel."

I, too, will be a dead mother with a son who's a writer. She worries about Hugo. She worries when she sees him staring at young men as if he had no idea what he looked like. As if no-one had ever told him that men his age don't dress like this. She worries when she recognises the longing in his eyes. It makes her feel helpless. It makes her want to walk away. If she'd been beautiful all her life her son wouldn't be like this. She should never have relied on Philip to give him everything; not that she would have done any better. She wants to say sorry.

"I don't like what he writes," she says.

"You've read his books?"

"Of course I've read his books," she says. "I told him I didn't like them."

"What don't you like about them?" he says.

115

"You know what I don't like," she says.

The narrator is a cross-dressing PI with a Puerto Rican boyfriend who's a medical student and a go-go dancer; they are cultural heroes. Heda Beilin's son's books have a cult following. Hugo laps them up, in secret. He knew Martin as a boy and looks for familiar faces amongst his characters. They'd gone to temple with their fathers and sat knees touching on Rosh Hashonah and Yom Kippur. Martin was fifteen when Hugo went off to college. He saw him again, years later at his father's funeral, standing so close to his Latino boyfriend Hugo couldn't make out his face, just his hands, like a ballet dancer's, talking to his mother.

"At the funeral?" Hugo says. "Is that where you spoke to him?"

"The critics love him," she says.

"He must be loaded," Hugo says.

"He came looking for you after the *shiva*," his mother says.

Hugo had this fantasy about making millions. The government would send a man to talk to him; to offer to fund his research, set him up in his own lab. His work would play a vital role in developing new ways of utilising the aerodynamics of traditional weaponry for sophisticated warfare. But then, Hugo would usher the man out, look straight into his blue eyes, and say: If there's anything you want to know, you'll find it in my book. Hugo was a pacifist. And for weeks afterwards he'd keep expecting the man to come back, to be impressed by his ideals, and to insist on making love to him.

"Are you going to write another one?" his mother says.

"I'm not interested in doing another one," he tells her. "I'm happy teaching."

"Don't you have to publish in that place?" she says.

"I'm too old," he says. "I haven't got another book in me."

116

"Nonsense," his mother says. "Stop doing that to yourself."

She finishes her coffee and folds the napkin into a triangular pillow. A lump, the doctor had said. A lump. A lump at your age is nothing out of the ordinary. That's the end of me, she thinks. What she's too scared to think is: What use will Hugo be if I become another Ada Blumberg? How easy it was for her children to leave her to Ada's own devices.

The men are drinking herbal tea and eating fruit salad. Hugo tries to make out the title of the man's book. He'd like to be surprised. He'd like someone as splendid as this to be reading Descartes or *Tristes*, then he'd have a chance. They'd have things to talk about, naked, the man's long hair on Hugo's chest after making love, at home in New York; on the porch at their beach house; holidaying in London in the fall. They'd be the perfect couple, have perfect friends, perfect conversations. Such gorgeous shoulders and armpit hair make Hugo wish his mother would give birth to him all over again.

"Are you going away this year?" she says.

"Away?" he says. "Where to? I can't afford to go away."

"I can't remember the last time I went on holiday," she says.

The coffee at the bottom of her mug is cold and she turns to the waiter, miming for a refill. She likes her coffee hot. When the waiter gets to the table she says no to the cream, but asks for cold milk. Her son covers the rim of his mug with an open palm.

"You were with Helen over Christmas," he says. "Wasn't that a vacation?"

"You know what I mean," she says. "A holiday holiday. A proper holiday."

When her husband had died she'd sold his practice and gone travelling to Paris, and the Caribbean, visited her

117

grandparents' graves in Warsaw. She went with friends until they started dying. She loved travelling with other women. Why she never started earlier, she'll never know. Maybe you're not meant to go away with the people you love; she didn't like going away with Philip. She wants to say this to her son. She knows he'd have something to add. She heard him and Eric arguing once over where to go on holiday. Eric liked museums; Hugo wanted to spend his time away from work in a white-washed cottage on a secluded beach.

"Will you be staying for dinner?" the waiter asks.

He's at the head of their table, witnessing everything. Hugo detects a smirk in his tone. Sometimes they stay for a light meal, especially in winter when it's nice to be cooked for. Now it's hot and sticky and Hugo wants a fruit salad of his own. He wants cool lumps of pineapple and kiwi fruit in his mouth. He wants to be on the beach in Naxos eating watermelon and feta cheese.

It pains her to see how uncomfortable he is. Lounging like a slob, ignoring the waiter. Maybe they should go home, but his house is so far from hers. One minute they're here; the next they'll be heading off in opposite directions.

"I'm going to have a fruit salad," he says. "Do you want anything?"

"Fruit salad?" she says. "Are we starting with dessert?"

"I'll just have a fruit salad," he says to the waiter.

"I'll eat when I get home," she says.

The waiter claws the coffee mugs with one hand and stuffs the napkins into them. He wipes the table and takes away the saucer. If Hugo could just block her out and enjoy his fruit salad, he'd soon be home.

She keeps remembering.

The dinner he took her to, the fundraising ball with the

118

English explorer who came to talk about his new book. They sat at a table with young academics; how amused she'd been by the 'Professor and Mrs Painter' calligraphed onto their place tag. He got upset, angry at the incompetence, what with him having organised the whole event. Her son was gone from the table most of the evening. Every so often she'd catch him running across the hall, speaking to people, looking admired, holding his stomach in. They'd had rice for dinner. Rice and chicken.

"They had fruit at that dinner," she says.

"Which dinner was that?" he says, wiping the dampness the waiter's cloth had left on the table's surface.

"That anthropology one," she says. "They had melon and prosciutto for starters, remember?"

Another man that had come and gone. She knows exactly what this is doing to him. That spite of hers is relentless. Carl had covered the water with magnolia petals and fed him fruit salad in the bath. He'd called him professor and rested his back against Hugo's chest. His hair was brown and blonde and his forehead — a vast, smooth slope. When they moved in the water, ripples washed over the sides and made soft noises as they splashed onto the tiles. Hugo had combed Carl's hair with his fingertips, they'd talked about AIDS and ex-boyfriends. Hugo told him he was ready to write another book; no arrows this time, he said; he wanted something more fluid. Carl had turned his head to look up at Hugo, and said: It's such a relief to find someone who doesn't care about gym tits and body piercings. He said to Hugo: Write a book about love.

"Do they still have those annual dinners?" she says. "Your father would have liked them."

"He'd have been bored out of his mind," Hugo said.

"He would have loved to see you," she said. "He would have been so proud."

119

"Please, mother," he says.

"Okay, I'm sorry," she says.

The man is staring at him. Talking to his boyfriend and looking right at Hugo. If his mother wasn't here, Hugo would get up now and go to the bathroom; he'd stand at the urinal, taking his time, unbuttoning his trousers and pissing and closing them again, washing his hands, and in the time it took to do all that, and to dry them, he'd know whether the man really wanted him. There was only that once, that one time with Eric, that he'd had sex in a toilet; the night they'd gone dancing and locked themselves in a cubicle to snort coke and fuck.

"I'll be back in a minute," Hugo says, because he has nothing to lose.

Sitting on her own at that dinner, prodding the slices of melon, she'd heard them talking about her son. The lecture was about to begin and people were moving back to their seats. She could tell, from the tone in the man's voice, that she wasn't going to like what he said. It wasn't the first time she'd overheard people talking about him. He was a boy when they started saying things behind his back, making fun of him. So she turned the place tag facedown and tilted her head to listen.

"He was my teacher at UCLA," the young man said. "He was funny. Remember the weird book he wrote about arrows?"

"He lost it after that," his friend said.

"He was a great guy," the former student said. "I'm going to go up and introduce myself."

She stood up then, took her bag and coat, and marched towards her son. He was telling a young student how to set up the book-signing table. He'd always been pudgy. Except for the years he'd lived with Eric, who'd made him go to the gym and stop eating in between meals. When Eric died, Hugo let himself go and called to say he was moving

120

back to New York. She'd gone to the funeral, but he wouldn't let her stand with him, so she'd landed up talking to a married stockbroker friend of Eric's. That was the last time she'd met any of his friends; she must ask him who his friends are now. She wants him to have lots of friends, not end up like her with whatever's going to happen and only Ada Blumberg to speak of.

Hugo comes back to the table in Chez Laurent without looking left or right, as if there is nothing he wants to see.

"Their toilets are always so clean," he says.

"You forgot to tuck your shirt in," his mother says.

"I prefer it this way," he says. "It's cooler."

"I wish you'd meet someone like Eric," she says. "I miss him."

"Ma, please," Hugo says.

"But you're still young," his mother says. "Aren't there nice people in the Village?"

That first summer in New York had been perfect. Everything was familiar. There were moments when he forgot about Eric and the year of his dying. He got involved in college politics and fundraising committees, started looking around for new ideas for a book. Coming back to New York had been the right move. Hugo was getting stronger. People respected his work. So when the fundraising ball came up, and the committee agreed to invite Bruce Chatwin to be the guest speaker, Hugo had asked his mother if she wanted to come along. And then she'd wanted to walk out before it even started.

"Go and sit down," he'd said.

"Do they all know you're gay?" his mother had said. "Does everyone know about you?"

"What are you talking about?"

"I think I'd rather go home," she'd said, moving away from his hand in the hollow of her back.

"Look, mother, I'm coming to sit down; the lecture's

about to start."

"I'd like to go home," she'd said. "I've had enough."

"We can't go now," he'd said. "I have to stay for Bruce."

"I'm going," she'd said. "You can stay."

And he did. He went back to the table and the young man who'd been his student was sitting in his mother's chair. That was Carl. They were never two men in vests and gym-toned bodies drinking carrot juice. They were never mistaken for twins. They were perfect; opposites attracting. They'd gone out for drinks that night, and when Carl went to the bathroom Hugo had called his mother; she had a headache and was getting ready for bed. She was missing his father, she'd said. When he put down the phone, Carl was standing next to him, so close Hugo had to let him lick his neck and kiss him. Three months later his mother had met Carl and they'd all come to Chez Laurent for coffee and macaroons.

"Strawberries!" his mother says. "What gorgeous strawberries."

"Have one," Hugo says, pushing the dish of fruit salad towards her.

"Have you heard from Carl?" she says, picking up a strawberry with her nails.

"Carl?" he says. "Oh, yes, Carl. He's in Boston, I think. He got tenure there."

Hugo had taken the train to Boston, and Carl had visited him in New York. It had been an adventure. Then Hugo had said it was disorienting for him and he didn't know if he could wait until Carl found a job in New York; all this to-ing and fro-ing was upsetting him, he needed security. He needed to know there was a future to look forward to.

"Don't you understand," he'd said to Carl. "I've already got one dead lover."

Carl kept up his weekend visits until Hugo came up with his ultimatum. They were sitting on a bench by the pond in Central Park eating sushi. Carl spat on the ground and called Hugo a pathetic, spiteful, self-loathing old queen. Then he got up and walked away.

"What a nice man," his mother says.

Hugo wants to be sick when she asks him questions about the men he's loved. She fills him with shame when she watches him like that. He's always hated bringing friends home. Even as a boy, she'd watch him play, judging desires in him he hadn't even named. And when he started dating men she'd invite them for dinner, she liked their company, she said, the company of men, especially after the divorce. It was after his father had died that they started coming here. Hugo's body cowers when she sees him so close to younger men. Fifteen years older than Carl. Probably twenty between him and the two by the mirror, reading, making idle chatter, writing away in their notebooks.

"Do you know those men?" his mother says.

"God, no," he says. "Why would I know them?"

"You're looking at them," she says. "You look as if you know them."

"I don't," he says.

"I can't see that far, but they look very handsome," she says. "Do you think they're gay?"

"God, mother, of course they're gay," he says.

Sometimes he wishes he knew more about her, wishes she was one of those mothers who liked to reminisce about her youth and her growing up. She'd never even taken him or his sister back to the part of London where she grew up. He imagined a dark secret that kept her quiet about the past. A violent father, a boyfriend who had left her for someone else. Sometimes he wishes that everything between them could be different. He would tell her everything and they'd be friends, just two old people. He wouldn't have to hide anything from her. Like when you went to the clap clinic in the seventies, or on the AIDS wards in the eighties. No secrets. Eric had told him things about the other patients; no-one had the energy to keep things to themselves. He wondered what Eric was telling the others about him: that he was controlling and always dissatisfied? that he'd written a book? was a well-known anthropologist? that he had a big penis? Eric always talked about Hugo's cock to his friends.

"How's the fruit salad?" his mother says.

"It's all apple at the bottom," Hugo says.

"We can go when you've finished," she says. "I'm getting hungry."

She knows what's best for him. She knows how much he can handle. Again she has rescued him from sharing the unmentionables. She doesn't want to know, and he'll gain nothing by telling her. Just once he'd shared his longing with her. They were on vacation in Viareggio. His sister had had an Italian boyfriend called Massimo and the three of them would go cycling in the woods by the beach. The two boys became friends and would laugh at each other's attempts to communicate through the Italian phrase-book Hugo had found at a second-hand bookshop near his father's surgery. When he realised Massimo would never love him, he'd cried to his mother, and she'd said: Don't put all your eggs into one basket, Hugo. Make sure you have lots of friends.

"I'm done," he says. "I've still got a lot to do before tomorrow."

There'll be other opportunities to tell him about the lump. She turns to catch the waiter's eye and smiles and nods for the check. How is she ever going to tell him? This will need more rehearsing than she expected. She slides

Hugo's fruit-salad bowl towards her and eats the cubes of green apple with his spoon.

"They're very sweet," she says.

He can't bear to listen. All those things he knows she's always wanted to say to him, to put him down, to keep him a baby, to insist he be perfect. All her silences, and the memories of his that she keeps bringing back to life, filling him with all the men he's loved and moved away from. Not one of them has stayed in his life. Not one of them has tried to make contact, come knocking at his door to be let back in. For all he knows, Carl could be living round the corner writing his own books on love. Could he tell her something? Isn't there something he could give her before they go home? Is it going to be like this until the end; she filling him with shame, he accepting disgust as if it were a second skin? He takes fifteen dollars from his wallet, ready to put them on the saucer when the check arrives.

"I'm just going to the bathroom," his mother says.

"I'll wait for you outside," Hugo says.

The other men are leaving, too; they're all going to get to the door at the same time.

"Hugo, is it?" the man with the book says. "Hugo Painter?"

Hugo wonders if he's a student, someone he's slept with, a colleague whose face he can't place. The man frowns at him and moves to get the door.

"It's Michael," the man says, raising his eyebrows as if pointing to himself, letting Hugo, then his boyfriend, through the door. "Michael Meltzer," he says. "A friend of Eric's."

"Michael," Hugo says, frowning.

"My brother was in hospital with Eric," he says. "I haven't seen you in ages. How are you?"

"I'm fine," Hugo says. "How's your brother?"

"Fine," the other man says, "I'm fine," and he smiles.

"I miss Eric."

"You look great," Michael says to Hugo, rays of laugh-lines spreading out from his eyes, running his hand through his thick hair. Hugo thinks of the word luxuriant. "Let's get together some time."

"Get together?" Hugo says.

"Yeah," says Michael. "I'd like that."

He takes his wallet out of his back pocket and gives Hugo his business card. They shake hands and the two men move away from Hugo. He wants to laugh, an hysterical kind of laughter full of relief and a sense of arrival. But he stands there on the sidewalk while the last light of the evening sun turns the office buildings to gold. The air is cooler now.

"I had a feeling you knew them," his mother says.

"They're friends of Eric's," Hugo says.

Now he is alone with his mother. Michael and his brother have walked off, but they turn, and everyone waves. Hugo keeps his hand in the air and hails a cab for his mother, who lets him hug her before she gets in. She is so careful not to overdo things; she doesn't want him to worry.

"It's been a lovely afternoon," she says, patting his back.

She won't tell him yet what the doctors said. There'll be time for that.

"I'll call you next week," he says, closing the cab door for her.

On the train, Hugo wishes he didn't have to tear up Michael's number. They'd have things to talk about; first about Eric, then other things. Hugo would be so proud to have a good-looking man with him again. They'd be in love and Hugo wouldn't be afraid. But then Passover would come along or Christmas or some High Holy Day and they'd all have to meet up and go to his mother's for din-

126

ner. She'd want to know everything. Hugo can't risk having Michael's number branded on his memory, so he tears up the card without looking at it, holding the scraps, pinched between his thumb and index finger, like pieces of a puzzle, ready to be thrown away when he steps out onto the platform.

THE GOOD OUTSIDE

Now that all the others have said their goodbyes and gone home for the night, Peter and David sit alone in the garden. Eventually they'll begin to talk about Jonathan. David will start, Peter will be reluctant. He'd rather sit quietly for a while and then head off to bed. To the sofa, in fact. He hasn't slept much since leaving Italy and it's been a hot day in the garden. But now with everyone gone until tomorrow, the air seems fresher. Twilight takes the edge off the lingering heat.

Cushions and mattresses are scattered across the lawn and a low coffee table has been set up under the apple tree. Someone had brought it outside for those sitting in the shade by the fish pond. This was Jonathan's garden. He had tomatoes and zucchini growing along one wall, gooseberries along the back, and honeysuckle up the other side and around the small patio where David and Peter are now sitting. Their table is covered with dirty mugs, glasses and plates; everything needs to be cleared away and tidied before people come back in the morning.

The second day of the *shiva* has been long and drawn-out. Peter spent most of the day, like the day before, gathering up as much news as he could. It had been ten years since he left Port Elizabeth for Italy. He'd left South Africa as soon as he thought of himself as a painter, and being an abstract artist, he believed he carried his inspiration inside him, that his work didn't depend on a landscape. He left South Africa to get away from death and from politics. At first he'd had a lover, Gianni, and then it was just himself in the small flat he'd bought outside Florence with the money his mother had left him.

Peter had been watching David from the moment he'd arrived at their house, hoping to catch memories of

129

Jonathan in his gestures, even if David was so much thinner than Jonathan, and taller; David had the grace of a dancer. It made Peter feel sluggish. He watched David greet people with a smile that was both pained and grateful, like in-laws accepting gifts for the bride and groom at a wedding they'd rather not be at. He watched David cry, and saw him being comforted by friends and by Jonathan's mother. It was only when David was quiet, alone, physically present but his mind elsewhere; when he was sitting like that on a cast iron chair, legs folded, elbows on the arm-rests, that Peter saw Jonathan in him. David had been with Jonathan for as long as Peter had been away.

David had caught Peter staring at him throughout the day. He could tell Peter knew he was keeping something from him. He felt sorry for Peter, and saw how he longed to be told how important he'd been to Jonathan. But David couldn't lie to him. He didn't have to; Peter wasn't *his* friend. He watched Peter trying to get people to talk to him. He noticed how he listened. Jonathan had told him that if anything, Peter was a good listener. But then someone would come up to David and hug him, sit by his side for a while, talk, and then go off to join one of the groups in the garden.

The larger group, made up mainly of Jonathan's friends, had spent the day at the edge of the garden under the apple tree. Peter sat with them most of the time, he knew some from their school days. Every so often a shriek or muffled giggle would come from the group, and if David turned to look, someone would point into the apple tree by way of an explanation and an apology. Another group had stayed nearer the round table on the patio, near David, close to the food.

Peter and David are sitting at that table in silence, each slowly moving away from being part of a gardenful of people to being alone together, something that hasn't

130

happened much over the past ten years. As far as Peter can remember, he's never been alone with David. He wants to say: It's a beautiful house the two of you made. But David speaks first.

"Do you know," he says "our Jonathan…"

Peter imagines he's about to tell him that Jonathan had left him something.

"…was a fucking slut," David says, throwing his head back and laughing.

"A slut?" Peter says, keeping a straight face.

"All day I've felt these secrets hovering in the garden. Like ghosts, or butterflies."

"What secrets?" Peter says.

"Was it just me?" David says. "Or did he keep secrets from everyone?"

"Not from me," Peter says.

Peter and Jonathan had been in kindergarten together, the Summerstrand Hebrew Nursery School. They'd known each other since they were two bricks and a piss-pot high, as Jonathan's mother, Mina, kept telling people. They'd go snake-hunting in the *veld* behind the Greek grocers and comb the dunes opposite Peter's house on Jenvey Road for bits of broken clay. They went to the same junior school, and in high school Peter was head boy and Jonathan his deputy. They were a good team. They could be kids again, playing sheriff. They told each other everything.

"So you knew all about this, did you?" David says.

"About what?" Peter says.

"All these strange little affairs he was having."

There was that period of five years when they went off to university: Jonathan to become a doctor; Peter to study art. They'd written lively, graphic letters to each other and spent three of the five summers together in PE. The other two summers they'd travelled abroad: Jonathan to

131

Europe; Peter to his mother's family in Israel.

"It was probably during those trips that the secrets began," David says.

"What secrets?" Peter says. "He always told me everything when he got back."

"So you did know, then," David says.

Peter could have given examples, and he was tempted to. But Jonathan had made him swear never to tell anyone. Not about the sex he'd had with two eighty-year old men in Paris. In a café near the Eiffel Tower he'd got chatting to a beautiful Moroccan boy who sold sex to men in old-age homes. They were so old, Jonathan told Peter, they smelt like his grandfather. And not about the arrest on the other trip, this time to London, where he'd been caught in the toilets on Leicester Square sucking someone's cock.

Jonathan told Peter everything in elaborate detail. They lay on his bed, Jonathan's bags still unpacked, the duty-free bottle of whisky almost empty, laughing hysterically and waggling their legs in the air like upturned cockroaches. Jonathan went to fetch more ice from the kitchen and on his way back stood over the bed and said: "Don't you ever tell anyone about this." And Peter said: "I swear. Cross my heart." And when, some years later they'd laughed again about these incidents, just before Peter went off to Italy, David already in the picture, Jonathan had made Peter swear again never to tell a soul.

"I don't know anything you don't know," he says.

"Then why are you so silent?" David says.

"Am I?"

That wasn't all Peter knew about Jonathan. He knew about the bad patch. Jonathan had found out about an affair David was having with a young Afrikaner and had played on David's Catholic guilt. David believed adultery was a sin, and that hell was a real place. And in all their years together, Jonathan had never told David about his own infidelities. He used David's one slip to keep the accusing finger pointed away from him. Unbeknownst to David, Jonathan used to write to Peter in Italy about cruising on Donkin Hill and landing up in strangers' beds. Just two years ago there'd been the black guy who'd taken Jonathan to his room in the Greek Orthodox church where his mother worked. He was a school teacher near Benoni. Jonathan had said they were thinking of coming to Europe after the elections.

"I hate being left in the dark," David says. "I hate that he's dead and can't tell me anything."

"Let's go inside?" Peter says. "Let's get this stuff into the kitchen."

In the ten years David had been with Jonathan, he'd barely heard him say one good word about Peter. David had been dreading this evening. He hadn't expected Peter to come to the funeral. Then he'd hoped Peter would be delayed in Italy, or have an exhibition he couldn't get away from. He'd met Peter a few times before he left South Africa, but he knew him mainly from Jonathan's stories, how they'd go out drinking and Jonathan would land up consuming more than he'd intended, then sharing things with Peter he'd meant to keep to himself. The truth was that at the time no-one knew him like Peter did and there was no-one else to confide in. He told David that his relationship with Peter had no room for small talk; he said it proudly at first, and then as if it was a burden.

"He's heavy," Jonathan had said. "Heavy and abstract. Even with alcohol."

David and Jonathan were relieved when Peter left for Italy. Jonathan would write to him occasionally, always in response to one of Peter's long, ruminative letters. David wanted to be the one Jonathan confided in. He was a writer, after all, and writers knew how to listen.

"What about big secrets?" David says. "I mean, how many secrets can a man have? You'd think that after ten years I'd know them all."

"It's the in-between secrets that are the tricky ones," Peter says. "The little indiscretions people think they've already shared with lovers, but somehow forget to mention. The tiny things that slip our minds because they're there all the time. It's like you don't tell your lover about your birth marks. He can see them."

"He loved telling secrets," David says.

"Yes," Peter says. "He did. Other people's secrets."

"It's too soon," David says.

"What is?"

They're discussing him in the past tense, fighting over him like vultures. Tearing him apart as if that, like Bacchus, would keep him alive.

David had insisted the *shiva* be held at their house. And because it was summer, almost Christmas, and they had no air-conditioning, they'd had the *shiva* in the small, clean, well-kept garden. Things hadn't gone smoothly. Jonathan's father had walked out that morning.

"Solly wasn't happy," Peter says.

David sits upright in his chair, hands on hips: "I will not have this turned into a garden party."

"Jonathan would have loved that," says Peter.

Jonathan's mother had tried to persuade her husband to stay, but he wouldn't listen. She'd followed him through the house to the front door, stopped to watch him march down the road to get the car. She'd have stayed if he hadn't driven up to the front door and said: Are you coming? David was standing behind her in the kitchen, putting cheese and crackers onto a tray, and she'd turned to him, embarrassed, then kissed him on the cheek.

"They'll come back tomorrow," David says.

"Call them," Peter says. "I probably remember their

number off by heart."

"They've all changed since you left," David says.

"Everything's changed," Peter says. "And nothing has."

The sky is strips of purple and navy blue and dark pink clouds. Peter notices how deep the colours are in the garden. Oranges and purples and whites, bold against the chrysanthemum leaves. The sweet-pea blossoms are beginning to brown, and the tomatoes are over-ripe, the zucchini too heavy. Jonathan would have picked and cooked them the weekend they took him to the hospital to die.

"Part of you does disappear when they go," David says. "It doesn't matter how prepared you are."

Peter's not going to share anything with David. He cannot bring himself to say: I envy the closeness you achieved. I can't imagine how you'll survive. I think about Gianni almost every day, even after five years. And he's not even dead.

"I'm giving his clothes to charity," David says.

"What for?"

"I don't want to see people I know wearing them."

Now, David is sitting in his chair like Jonathan, surveying the garden, a little detached, like Jonathan used to do when he was in doctor mode, the air of aloofness that the power to diagnose gives one, not unlike being a writer. Peter has also adopted a way of being, a way of sitting that fits the reclusive artist he has become; slouched, indifferent, as if unaware of his size and the way his curls fall across his face.

"What happened to Simon?" Peter says.

"He'd know what to do with the clothes," David says.

Simon is a fashion designer.

"He did call earlier," Peter says.

"Did I speak to him?" David says.

"Let's get something to eat," Peter says.

"I'll give his shirts to Simon," David say. "He made most of them."

Peter hasn't see Simon since moving to Italy. He never knew Jonathan had kept in touch. Maybe there were secrets. About five years ago, when Jonathan came to visit him in Italy soon after Gianni moved out, he told Peter about the Saturday mornings him and Barry Sher used to go oyster-hunting in the rock pools in Summerstrand and sell them for twenty cents a dozen to the Marine Hotel. And even though thirty years had passed, he felt left out and jealous.

How awkward Jonathan would have felt seeing Peter and David together in his small garden, chatting away. The three of them had hardly ever been alone together, except when Peter had had a boyfriend before he left for Italy, and then he and the boyfriend were invited for dinner at David and Jonathan's.

"Steve called from Jo'berg," Peter says.

"You should have let me speak to him."

"Why him?"

"He's your ex," David says. "That makes him part of the family."

"Hardly," Peter says.

"I liked Steve," David says.

"He went back to that wife of his," Peter says.

"Then left her again," David says.

The garden will be filled with people tomorrow. Peter will have old friends to gather more news from. There'll be Simon to fill him in, and Jonathan's mother to remind him of when he was a boy. He needs all this to take back to Italy.

"Do you want something to eat?" says Peter.

"Maybe just a little something," David says.

"Like what?" Peter says.

"Maybe some of those cheese things," David says.

"I've been thinking about them," Peter says.

"I tasted one when she brought them," David says. "They're perfect."

"Let me get the whole tray," Peter says.

Peter goes into the house and is glad to be alone. The lights are still off, so he makes his way through the house from memory. He leans against the kitchen doorway. He had helped Jonathan take the door down when he moved in. He could still see where the hinges had been screwed off, the holes covered up with Polyfilla, and then painted. Even after David had moved in, and was asleep upstairs, they'd come back to Jonathan's kitchen at the end of a night out. Now Peter walks in and bumps his hip against the butcher's block that wasn't there when Jonathan moved in.

"They're on top of the fridge," David says, switching on the kitchen light.

"What's that?"

"I hid them," David says.

Peter takes the plate of cheese sticks and avocado dip, and gets serviettes from the drawer by the sink.

"Still the same drawer," he says.

"You know what's frustrating?" David says, opening the fridge and taking out a bottle of wine. "I can be angry at him all I like and it won't make a difference."

"No," Peter says.

"His father won't talk to me about him," David says. "Mina does. But I want the stories from him. It feels like he's punishing me. You tell me about Jonathan."

"I hadn't heard from him in ages. You know that. I've had one letter from him in the past two years, and then it was just to tell me he was ill. He stopped answering my letters. Why?"

"This is not the way it should be," says David.

137

"Why did he stop writing?" Peter says.

"I don't know, Peter," David says, holding the wine bottle in both hands. "I really don't. I just don't want to feel so empty."

Peter puts down the plate and serviettes and opens his arms for David. David frowns at him.

"Please don't make me cry," he says.

Peter takes the wine bottle from David and puts it on the counter. He holds him and David cries into his shoulder. Peter's body turns to stone and with his eyes wide open he looks over David's shoulder. He stares blankly through to the garden where the man who one day will love him is standing. That man is waiting for Peter to come to him, having seen how bravely he holds this man's grief. That man will comfort Peter.

David smells of sweat and two-day old after-shave. He isn't going to shave or wash during the *shiva*. Jonathan's mother had told him yesterday morning while they covered the mirrors with scarves and pillow-cases that it was only the shaving he shouldn't do, but David wanted to prolong the way he'd been when Jonathan was alive. He wants his mourning to have Biblical proportions, to stay true to the pairing of their names. His body trembles in Peter's arms, and Peter becomes a life-time's worth of goodbyes to him. David feels so empty he could scream.

Five years ago, when Peter had driven Jonathan to Rome airport to catch the plane back to South Africa, they'd hugged in the waiting lounge, and Peter had cried then like a little boy being abandoned. Jonathan had held Peter's cheeks in his palms and for the first time ever kissed him on his mouth, full, letting his tongue linger against Peter's. Then he got on the plane and Peter went back to his flat, back to speaking Italian to everyone, back to finding ways to translate his demons into forms and colours. That's what he relied on. He is grateful to have

138

David's fists pressing into his back.

David feels like a stranger in a foreign country, feels himself getting smaller and smaller. This isn't his house anymore. From the moment Peter walked in, it stopped being home. This is how he used to feel when Peter spent the night here after his and Jonathan's drunken binges. This is why David always made sure he was asleep before they got back. Knowing Jonathan longer made the house more Peter's than his; Peter's images of Jonathan go back to a time before David, so he digs his fingers into Peter's back and opens him like stage curtains.

"What am I going to do?" David says.

He loosens his grip on Peter's back, and Peter is left alone.

"Let's eat," Peter says, stepping back.

"And drink," David says, taking the bottle of wine.

Back in the garden David makes room on the table for the wine and the glasses and the plate of cheese sticks. Then he pours wine into the glasses, and they wish each other long life, as is the custom.

THE THINGS YOU SAY
WHEN YOU SAY GOODBYE FOREVER

Dean is in Paris with his mother. He wants time and space to think about things, which is fine by me, because I need time and space, too. I wanted to say to him: How will you ever know what you want with your mother so close to your body? But then I remembered who she was, what she'd done for him, and I said: I feel as if I'm grabbing at bits of you before you slip away. Dean tells me I can end the relationship if I want to; he's not going to be the one to say goodbye. I shiver so much I can't talk, and he says: Why do you have to be so emotionless?

Now, sitting in the shade of the apple tree in my back garden, the open air is a relief after being cooped up in my room for what feels like weeks. Summer holidays are a trying time for grown-ups, even those of us without children. Three more weeks before I go back to teach. Or maybe I won't. This devotion to the needs and well-being of others has made me angry and unkind; it leaves me little time to remember who I am.

Maya calls from Cape Town just as I am about to leave for La Cucina, my late-morning Sunday café in Soho. We talk about the difference between 'anxiety' and 'depression.' I say I hardly ever feel anxious in my room, yet it's there that I am most in touch with, and able to bear my depression. What is our motivation? Maya says. What do we get up in the morning for? And we concede: We're here to find beauty. When we lived in the same country I played Orpheus to her Eurydice. When our lovers were away we'd eat sweet-and-sour pork ribs with fresh asparagus and drink white wine with mango ice-cream. Now we talk about Adam and Eve and the inevitable stage in each relationship when the apple gets eaten and there's no place to hide from the truth. She asks if this is about me and her or about Dean and I.

"It's about everyone," I say.

And we laugh, because she knows me like anyone knows and forgives the person who has watched them in hell. She tells me that since I left to live in London she hasn't had anyone to talk to. She says she hates London because London has me. She knows I will never come back. Even if here, too, I am a foreigner, impoverished of memory and desire, left only with the language I learnt about the world in. At least you've got that, the ancestors say, on the boat from Vilna to Cape Town, taking the family story from one continent to another. London is the closest I'll ever get to home.

"And who's going to cook me nice things?" she says.

I take the 73 bus to Tottenham Court Road and walk down Charing Cross to La Cucina. There's an empty table by the window that is open onto the street. Sam, a friend of Maya's who moved to London long before I did, brought me here soon after I arrived. It was one of the only places you could sit for hours, undisturbed, on one cup of tea. A young Polish woman served us then; later I got to know an older peroxided waitress who'd taught English in Gdansk. Today there are two Italian-speaking Polish waitresses. There is a comfort in being served by others from other countries, and to sit amongst tourists and people from out of town, like the young Australian couple at the table on the pavement outside the window, who order a cappuccino and an iced coffee. He rolls a cigarette while they wait for their drinks; she looks through a brochure.

"How about this one?" she says.

"Is that what you'd like?" he says.

"Well, I'm not really sure what I'd like."

"Are you having second thoughts?" he says.

"Why?" she says. "Are you?"

He shakes his head and holds out his hand. She gives him the brochure — it's a catalogue of body piercings — and surveys the street, looking for stories to carry back home with her. A man who might be a pimp or a cab driver walks up and down the side-street outside the café eating a pistachio ice cream which diminishes each time he comes into view.

I don't know if I can face the journey back to Stoke Newington, so I walk up and down Shaftesbury Avenue to wear out the pain. I am my mother; she is in me and my heart is cold. The ice that comes and goes and freezes around my heart and inside my chest is back. When beauty looks me in the eyes I imagine telling him my life story, starting in the 1860s or thereabouts.

"Tell me more," he'll say. "And then come fuck me."

On the train from Leicester Square to Finsbury Park I read Hemingway's *Paris Review* interview. He says that painters have had a profound influence on his work, though he's not very good at explaining why. Writers envy painters, envy them their capacity to translate their dread and confusion into tangible images. Still, a coincidence to chance upon this after seeing the Hundertwasser exhibition with its intricate, mosaic-like, fragmented paintings, and reading about his obsession with his art. I want his kind of freedom; the kind that comes with taking off your clothes in a public lecture hall, and living in a caravan in a field in the middle of a strange country. And what about Hemingway's mother dressing him up in frilly frocks until he was five? What did Mrs Hundertwasser do to her little boy to make him the way he was? And Dean — just one more day in Paris — whose mother gave him away when he was three days old, just time enough to learn the smell of the body from which he came, before being passed on to the woman he will call mother.

By two in the morning electric currents are running through me screaming at my body to stay awake. I switch on my bedside lamp and go back to Hemingway. If a writer stops observing, he says, he's finished. And the ice around my heart begins to melt; I am not alone anymore; this constant gnawing at the world for sustenance is justified. I know Hemingway well enough to tell him I'm too scared to really stop and observe, too scared to trust my own built-in, shock proof shit detector, too scared to record exactly what I see. I'm not man enough for you, Papa, am I?

Filled with this realisation, a complete story, I am ready for sleep. The house is quiet.

* * *

I hate the summer when only one layer of clothing is possible and bearable. Clothes have always been my shield: they hide my sweat and fat and overgrown nipples. No, I can't write about all this yet. There's a limit to the amount of self-disgust one can expect others to contain. Lighten this up. So, *voila*: January is the kindest month. Jumper and coat time. Hat, glove, and long-john time. A time when the body forgets its anxieties of exposure. A time to crack open the thin layers of frost that seal in the puddles. A time to frolic and dance and throw watchamacallit to the wind.

Dean and I met in January at a guest house in Cricieth. We landed up at the same table for breakfast, our rooms were adjacent, we were the Londoners in the house. We'd both come to immerse ourselves in the beauty of nature. Beauty like this: Him and I walking along the path to the river, past the bramble and the ivy, through the turnstile and over the fence that keeps the bulls away from the stream. Walking close to the water, watching it slide over algae-covered rocks, and I remember thinking: It's like

144

we've been waiting a lifetime for this. It's like: before you know it, we're a we. We walk and the water flows over the rocks; the sound is what we feed on for the first nine months of our being. Water is the first sound we hear. Over the bridge and back though the grazing fields, holding hands, saying hello to villagers on the way. United in the world, my inner reality has no power to undermine this splendour. I can barely stop myself from laughing and singing and dancing like a Welsh forest sprite.

Back home again — long after Cricieth, it is the day after Dean returns from Paris — we cling to each other like two boys drowning. Dean says he's surprised how much the prospect of sex with me frightens him. I want to know: How can the beautiful be so scared of touch? With his well-toned muscles and sexually unambiguous jaw. His thick black hair and outrageously protruding nose, so deliciously unashamed of itself, his piano-playing fingers, his Caribbean-sea blue eyes, his muscular hairy legs, his long thick penis that sways when he walks because it is made of gold. If I looked anything like him, I'd stand on a stool with a sign around my neck saying: Touch Me. If Dean were to disappear I would be left with nothing. I sometimes think that I can only see myself as those who step into my field of vision.

"There's something brutal about you," he says.

"Me?"

"It's like nothing is ever enough for you," he says. "Like you're always trying to grasp things from everywhere. Like you deserve to snatch whatever you want from others, from the world."

In last night's dream Gertrude Stein walks along the path opposite my window in her dressing gown and sandals. I am in the cottage near Cricieth; Gertrude has a small hut to herself. She's just made some coffee in the communal kitchen and is taking it back to her room. The

145

air is cool with last night and the sun is behind the hills. Mist hovers like muslin on the grass. She stops, brings her mug to her lips, tests the waters, and walks on to her hut. Minutes later she returns, striding across the paved courtyard towards the kitchen door, head down, her dressing gown exposing lush chest hair. Then, back again, skipping up the stairs, prancing along the footpath, another mug in her hand. I hear a voice coming from her hut. Could it be Alice lying in bed, clipping her toe nails, waxing her moustache? And then, one final sortie, Gertrude comes back to the cottage, a pillow and a green towel tucked under her arm, Basket trailing behind her. I call: Gertrude. Gertrude. Ms Stein. But she keeps walking. Now I'll have to run down to the kitchen to show her what I've made.

* * *

How do you put the spider's web into words? How do you explain where each thread goes? Why doesn't the web break when the spider runs across it? What, in human terms, is the relation between the weight of the spider and the strength of its threads? I watch the spider's fouetté with the wasp before it nibbles out its flesh and chucks the remains onto the ground, then mends the hole in the centre of its web. A bee sucks pollen from the lavender flowers. I am a cat and the sun feeds my skin; I could curl up under the sage bush and sleep there forever. Which is when Stephen, one of my house-mates, calls me to the phone. It's Dean.

I mouth, "What does he want?" rolling back my eyes, feigning indifference.

Stephen shrugs, because he can't know. He has no idea what's been happening between Dean and I. No-one knows. Except my mother, who calls later and tells me nothing unthinkable happened in my childhood. She assures me she never locked me in a cupboard or beat me with a stick, if that's what I'm imagining. I tell her I just want to know why I feel so unworthy of love. She is sobbing now; the pain is too much for her to bear. I scream with no sound in my throat and my tears dry up and my sadness turns to stone.

"It's the empty nest syndrome," she tells me.

"It must be hard," I say.

"You haven't been home since the army," she says.

So I say: "You sent me there to be killed. How can I come home after that?"

"Are you ever happy?" she asks.

"When I'm sitting in the garden in the morning, yes," I say. "Are you?"

"No," she says.

I stay at home and cook lasagne for Dean and I. The ragu simmers for five hours like Marcella says it should. I make the béchamel sauce and the pasta. I make garlic bread with the loaf I've kept in the freezer from the batch of sunflower-seed bread I baked some weeks ago. I cannot think what to do for dessert. We're always too drunk and needy by the time we've finished our main course. I remember the relief in finding someone who could drink as much as I could, someone who could go to bars without pretending conversation or company were the main reasons to be there. I would make the chocolate mousse with orange zest, if I still had the recipe. Dean calls after seven to say he needs more time to think; he suggests we meet in the park on Tuesday evening.

"I know you've made dinner," he says.

"I'd rather we met here or at your place," I say.

"I'm scared," he says. "I told you about what happened with Otis."

The man who threw stones through his window and

147

screamed to be let back in — all this after Dean had told Otis he'd met an Argentinian waiter on the beach in Sitges, and was leaving him. And when Dean did open the door, Otis went round the flat smashing everything that could be hurled against a wall.

I eat my way through the lasagne and finish off the bottle of wine. Once, out of rage and frustration, I'd thrown a glass onto the kitchen floor, thinking, as it broke, how the movies never show you the subsequent cleaning up of the shards. I serve myself some chocolate ice-cream. I've enjoyed this act of self-nourishment. I've earned it. Besides, no-one makes a lasagne as magnificent as my own.

I could call Dean and say: "You see, the difference between you and me is that you never had much compassion for the needs of your inner child. You can't escape the scars inflicted on your mind and body since the day you were born."

"It's late," he'll say. "I need to sleep. Especially now. We'll talk on Tuesday."

I know there's something I can say to persuade him to stay and witness my love for him. I just have to think harder.

* * *

We meet up on Tuesday, neither here nor there nor in a public place. We go for dinner to Frank and Frank. We both get very drunk and on the way home in the back of the cab Dean asks me if I love him. I say: What does that mean? He says: See, you *are* cold inside. When we get into bed Dean screams and shakes as if someone is killing him and makes me swear never to leave him. I let him slide his head under my T-shirt and I stroke it until he falls asleep.

I think: If I'd fucked him the night we met we wouldn't be behaving like this. He'd be mine by now.

Six months since I met Dean and three weeks since he said he didn't know if he could cope anymore with my intensity. He said: You're going to have to lighten up if you want to be with me. All I could hear was my mother's voice: It's such a gorgeous day outside; go and play with the other boys. In the beginning my life with Dean took on the lightness that comes with promises for the future, now it is burdened with the weight of every past disappointment. I want to find a way to remedy that. I want to find beauty. Now.

* * *

I scratch the tips of my nipples with my nails until the ecstasy threatens to drive me mad and I want to wail from longing. I stop myself from coming, get drunk on gin, and go out looking for uncomplicated sex. I sit in the corner of Compton's Bar until a man called Mario comes to speak to me. He says I'm different from the other men in the pub; they're all queens, I'm a real man. That's my cue to perform, so I take his cock out, spit into my palm and, too drunk to care, begin to jerk him off.

"Is big, isn't it?" he says. "Is nine inches."

His hair is so thick it takes me a few seconds to find his arsehole. When last drinks are called, Mario invites me to join him in the toilet, where he holds my cock and makes me pee onto the walls and toilet seat. Then he pulls down his pants and gives me a condom.

"I can't," I say. "Not in here."

"Pleez," he says. "Jus to feeneesh."

So I lick two fingers and play with his arsehole until he comes on the toilet seat. I feel young and reckless and wonder if he might like to go dancing; I know a place in

Hoxton where they play soul and R&B. But he has to be at work for eight, so he tears off a square of toilet paper and writes down his phone number.

"You not have to," he says.

"But I want to," I say.

"You not call me," he says.

"I will."

"You too bizi," he says.

"Busy?" I say. "I'm not busy."

I fold the piece of paper and tuck it into my back pocket with my travelcard.

"You too bizi," he says. "You toll me."

"I told you?"

"You not call me," he says.

"I will."

"No," he says. "I know."

"Oh, Mario," I say, going down on bended knee. "Will you marry me?"

Dean comes over, uninvited, so I suggest we go for a walk. I will not get into a row over our different concepts of boundaries (one cannot turn up unannounced on a man's doorstep unless one is willing to be fucked, which Dean is not). We drive to Regent's Park and walk along the canal, and even though I suspect he's been having sex with other men in parks and public toilets, I listen to him name the birds in the pond; I enjoy his closeness to nature, the casual way he distinguishes between living things. I ask if anything happened in Paris, seeing as we've never actually, well, like, fucked. He tells me the Parisian men loved him; they bought him drinks and took him out to eat, though he swears he never went home with any of them. His mother was, he reminds me, waiting for him at the hotel.

"How come it's taken you so long to tell me all this?" I say.

"All I did was talk to them about you," he says. "I missed you all the time."

I don't tell him about Mario, because in no way does it reflect on who I am. I tell Dean that Cousin Jeremy is stopping over on his way back from Singapore to Chicago. I tell him stories about my family, thinking that these brief myths of my origin might keep him close to me.

"About last Tuesday," I say.

"Please," he says. "Not now."

* * *

This is what has been happening: 1) Cousin Jeremy arrived on Thursday. I went with him and his friends — one works for Warner Brothers, the other's in property development — for dinner at The Ivy. They spoke about white furniture and about Liza and Barbra. Cousin Jeremy said gay men without children are the only category of people who can have a white lounge suite. Dean worked late. 2) I spoke to my mother. 3) Dean spends nights working on his dissertation; he wants to prove that metaphors are masculine and similes feminine. 4) I spoke to my mother again. She says she's feeling fine, just great. 5) I'm still contemplating giving up teaching. 6) I go out to buy the Sunday papers at the newsagent on the High Street, and bump into John and his daughter, six-year old Rachel, my pupil.

We talk about sibling rivalry, and how, when Rachel's little brother Jack was born, he was too ill to come home and she and her daddy sat on the stairs outside the hospital, crying. I tell John how important it is to keep talking about that, to remind Rachel of that time. I tell him I'm not going back to teach.

"I'm leaving," I tell Rachel.

"I'm leaving, too," she says.

151

"Oh," I say. "Where are you going?"

"To the seaside," she says. "And you can come visit me."

Enough.

Where am I in all this, making up stories out of everything, trying to tell tales through a fog of self-hatred. Will I ever be able to tell plain and simple stories if my body keeps disgusting me to distraction? Every story is born in the body. And the soul? What about the soul? Well, my soul is a pea. Don't expect me to feed you. And don't be surprised if I erupt into a beggar's rage. Back at home I eat my way through two packets of sesame sticks from the health food shop on Church Street, then a fistful of mini-marshmallows that I melt in a mug of hot chocolate.

Dean calls as I'm going out into the garden — another Sunday ritual — to say he's on his way to see Big Frank in Crouch End. He wants to know if he can stop by to talk. I tell him all this stopping and starting is too painful for me; I can't keep track of who either of us is anymore. He says it's all he can offer at the moment. We agree to talk tomorrow night when he gets in from college.

I take the supplements from *The Observer* and *The Independent* and force myself to go to La Cucina, where the waitresses are ignoring me even though I always leave a 30% tip. I sit by the window and order a pot of Earl Grey tea and a small plate of star-shaped polenta and almond biscuits; they have the texture of a biscuit my mother used to make called Melting Moments, those crumbly biscuits she'd bake for evenings when her book club met at our house. As I browse through the newspaper magazines I notice they've installed a small television set in the corner above me, like a spider's web. So this is it; the Disney Channel has colonised one of the only places left to escape to. My world is shrinking.

Back out on the street, I dart around Soho like Beep-Beep the Roadrunner, sipping from a small bottle of Captain Morgan. I come to rest at Compton's Bar, its wondrous smell wrapping around me like a ghost. That essence of early autumn — lager, cigarette smoke, and wooden floors — of closed places where the elements combine to create the most welcoming of fragrances.

* * *

Gertrude Stein visited me again last night. This time she's in my mother's living room by the window overlooking the docks. She says: Don't you dare look at me. She says: If your eyes even touch me for one second you can forget it. You'll never get fucked by me.

Which is when her slave walks into the room — his eyes on me so not to look at her — and climbs over Gertrude to snuggle up with his back to her groin. I watch him close his eyes and purr like a cat. I smile at Gertrude, and she smiles at me, conspiratorially.

"It's not the realism that matters," she says. "It's the composition of it all."

Then she turns to her slave and inserts her penis into his smooth backside.

All the men I've loved remind me of my mother. The way they disengage, switch off, turn away when I'm about to cry. It's true. And it's also, as Maya keeps reminding me, just a little bit of projection. Dean and I talk on the phone for the last time.

I say: "Do you remember the beautiful things you said to me?"

"Like what?" he says.

"You said I was wise," I say. "And gorgeous and special. Do you remember when we lay on opposite sofas in the guest-house's living room, before we touched? Do you remember when you hurt your back the following morning and I put your socks on for you and tied your laces? Do you remember sitting with the other guests after lunch, and me passing you your mug of coffee because I could see how painful it was for you to move?

"Dean," I whisper, trying to sound sexy, restrained, thoughtful, ignoring the blood that is freezing inside me, "I wish I had the right words to make you not-scared. You know, on the train back to London, without you, my stomach was full of knots. I thought I would choke from longing."

Nothing has changed, I want to say, the pangs in my gut are still the excitement and disappointment of being connected to another person in the world. Like at the moment of birth.

I cannot maintain this level of grief.

"Do you think it's been any easier for me?" he says.

And then we say the things you say when you say goodbye forever on the phone.

THE LAST SOUTH AFRICAN

(This is a story I've wanted to get off my chest for a long time and haven't been able to find a way to begin telling it. Then a few days ago I came across something Jean Genet said. He said that writing is the last resort when you have betrayed. I came across his words in a book about a young Moroccan man growing up in Paris. The story reminded me of Majid, whom I haven't seen in a while, and of Becka. The story I want to tell is Becka's. It is the story of her day before the morning we met. She is at home in North London. Majid is at the bakery they own. I am... well, you'll see where I am.)

Becka picks up her baby from his cradle and takes him down the stairs into the conservatory. She loves the ease with which she carries him, a confidence gained from holding the babies of the Hasidic women she teaches. One of them had told her, just weeks before Becka took her leave to spend the last few afternoons in Stoke Newington's Church Street cafés reading romance novels, that the body stops you from letting go, just as it keeps you from sinning in your sleep, or jumping out of a window. Becka had looked it up, the hypothalamus, though Rivka-Surah had called it faith, like *Ha'Shem*, protecting even those parts of the body that are no longer part of it. Her baby's smell is perfect, of porridge, of warm milk, of sweet sweat and soap. Is this what they mean when they say: I could eat you up.

Just little bites, to nibble him back into her body. To become him. Becka wraps her baby up against her as she settles into the wicker armchair in the sun. The conservatory juts out into the garden and is filled with sun-warmth and the scent of rosemary and thyme that grows in the boxes on the ledge along the sides of the glass walls. In the garden, but protected from the cold spring air, the sun shines onto her face and shoulders and thaws her skin, opens it up like chocolate melting, ridding her of sharp edges and opposition. Everything around her is hushed, like an expectation.

Keep going, Becka tells herself.

The wicker chair squeaks under their weight. She listens to her own breathing, as if it hadn't been there before; her baby whimpers, laments: This is her music. She loosens her strap and opens the hatch of her bra; on her breast again and he's quiet and focused and oblivious. Magic. She smiles at the power she has to comfort him. Him. Who's him? Say it: Her son. Her son depends on her. The warmth, too, has erased the frustration at being kept awake all night and at Majid's reluctance to get up when prodded. The warmth, and being the world to someone in a way that arouses envy in Majid. Her feet on the coffee table with her baby in the cavity of her stomach: Becka stares at the hugeness of her nipple in his tiny mouth.

"That's better," she says, holding the nipple for him, making it easier for him to suck.

Her uncle is dead. The thought won't go away. Her baby looses his grip and frowns and whimpers. All because she sat down; but she couldn't keep moving around the house, dusting, making things neat and tidy, standing at the window like a housewife. It fills her body, this realisation of a death, as if life were being washed from her and poured back simultaneously. Very different to this when she got the news about her mother; then it was guilt or regret or pity; this time it's a taste of pure death, of dissolution and relief. Her baby is back on her nipple, tugging away.

"Let's try the other one, boo-boo" she says.

She has both shoulder straps undone and his hands

clamber across her chest to suck. The noises are adamant, relentless, sexual. It reminds her of her own mouth sucking on Majid's cock or him between her legs; she wants him on the floor, drinking from her. And then the consequences come to her — a joke, really — the having to give up her body and be taken over, the responsibility for another life that will be there forever, like she was to a mother who didn't want to know and went to live the life of an artist in a hut on the Transkei coast.

If she joined a mothers' group, would they all be having the same thoughts? What do new mothers think about? And her students, the procreating Hasidic women of Stamford Hill, how are they getting on with the *shikseh* woman Becka got to sub for her? Have they ever been so close to a tall blond girl from Yorkshire; and Lesley, how would she handle a class full of Jews? Had she ever been so close to so many. I'm on their side, Becka thinks, no different from the wigged masses, breeding away, my body doing what God intended.

"Who's my illegitimate baby?" she says, leaning over gently to make sure her nipple stays in his mouth, to kiss his forehead, her lips dry against his perfect skin.

His eyes are closed. They're brown, almost black, Jewish eyes; not the blue she was born with, passed down from the red-headed Cossack who'd raped her great-great-grandmother. Becka looks for signs of herself in her baby, which parts of hers were strong enough to push Majid's genes aside? Some days she sees her frown, when Majid points it out to her: "Stop frowning like that at him," he says. "You're teaching him bad habits." He'd given their baby his Sephardi skin and eyes, his thick dark hair; she likes to think she gave their baby his shape: his chin, his ears, his tummy, from which she now lifts his little T-shirt to blow drum-rolls on his skin.

157

Her aunt says it was prostate cancer — horrible medication that gave him massive breasts and pitched his voice so high he was embarrassed to talk. By the time he died, he'd lost all his desire and his voice was just a squeak.

Her baby whimpers and Becka puts him back onto her nipple. She wonders if all this is still her body, now that its function has changed, everything inside her altered. The months of being so full, stretched to the limit and possessed, had been a lifetime. How will her body ever forget that? The change came with the pregnancy, which she got used to, the way the body tries to adapt to a new organ, the way the mind accommodates the unexpected. Only now with him out of her, stuck to her nipple, the two of them alone in the house with no-one to remind her who she was, does she think she might do something disgusting to get him back inside.

"Your mommy has such silly thoughts," she says.

And strokes his head with the tips of her fingers; she doesn't want to distract him, his hair like dyed silk threads, black like Majid's and her father's side of the family. She plays with it casually, as if it were her own body, making patterns in his hair. His skull is clay hardening. Three months, and now a death that is threatening to disrupt this abandonment to her baby's needs. Her feet rest on the edge of the table-top as she rocks herself, keeping their bodies moving, trying to please her baby in every way possible. Becka uses his burping blanket to wipe the milk from her stomach and the sweat from under her breasts.

"I want to be the baby," she says, her nose close to his smell. His hair so soft, his skin wrinkled from the months of being in the waters of her insides, his eyes rolled back in his head, ecstatic, sucking to empty her out.

Majid appears with flour in his hair, white and wholemeal. They'd bought the bakery from an Israeli couple who were so sick of London they'd gone back to Jerusalem. He stands at the top of the conservatory stairs smiling at her, she can tell, because she is a mother, and he is still shy about being a father. She's not sure if this is reason enough to resent him, or whether, like the truth it is, she should accept it and smile back, let him know she has been waiting for him. Majid's beauty gets her every time. He leans against the doorway at the top of the stairs, his hands in his pockets, his faded blue T-shirt, like a kibbutznik's, loose on his body, just the outline of his nipples and the soft mound of his tummy. Still smiling, as if to say: "I have earned our daily bread; now I deserve to be loved."

"*M'sael cher*," he says, breaking the comfort of their silence.

"*M'sael nur*," she says, smiling back.

She reads it as trust when he speaks to her in Arabic. It's when he stays away from her for so long that her mind won't let go. Her love for him grows when he's away; when he comes back she blames him for this weakness, his fear of approaching her in large strides. Becka sits up in the armchair and lowers Samih onto her lap, her eyes there to meet his. Majid comes down into the conservatory, wipes his hands on his T-shirt, ready to touch her skin. The baby looks up at him; they're smiling at each other, Majid still unsure what words to use, what language, Arabic or English. With her, too, he's sometimes afraid to ask simple questions: How is he? Has he slept? Then he remembers it's his baby, too.

They'd met outside the Royal Festival Hall after a Middle Eastern concert. She'd been to see the Egyptian Sufi woman that Saturday afternoon, her first summer in London, still revelling in the freedom of being away from home. During the concert, she'd sat with her eyes closed and the music had filled her, found a place to settle inside as if her body remembered Arabian deserts from two thou-

159

sand years ago. Later, a warm evening in front of the building, Becka had stood at the wall overlooking the Thames. This was her succour in London: a river that had been here forever.

Majid served her falafel and taboulleh at one of the food stands, surprised when she spoke to him in Arabic. "Hardly more than *shukran*," she laughed. She told him she'd picked it up from some Palestinians she'd worked with on a farm in Israel before coming to London. She was surprised to find a Jew from Syria cooking for a living and playing the ud in a band of Egyptian musicians. And what made her think of this? That same evening she'd waited for him on a bench by the river outside the NFT café. She didn't have to wait long — his pots were soon empty — and she'd watched him walk down the stairs towards her, smiling.

Becka sees herself with Majid's eyes: Her legs on the table, the hem of her floral dress around her thighs, her shoulders bare and glowing, her hair tied back, loose strands on her forehead. How lucky he is, kneeling by the armchair to kiss her back, then her shoulder, running his fingertips over her arm, goosebumps rising on her skin, circling her elbow, and along the bone that leads to her hand, where he rests his open palm, hiding her fingers with his. He glides his hand cautiously onto Samih's head, like a snake over a rock, to smooth his hair and stroke his cheek.

Becka watches the soft hairs on Majid's knuckles, the dough in the folds of his skin, under his fingernails. His touch lingers on her body. He stares into Samih as if he were a crystal ball, not daring to look at her for fear of dispelling the magic, this illusion of fatherhood. Becka tells herself: Keep with him. He wants to love both of you. Doesn't that entitle him to your skin. But before she can let herself accept anything, she gets up, walks barefoot up the stairs to the kitchen; there's dinner to be served. She'd made the *kubbeh* Majid's mother had taught her — the lamb mince wrapped in cracked bulgur wheat — not long before she died in her Brighton flat, begging to be taken home to Syria.

Majid watches Becka's skirt unravel and cover her legs, his eyes on her back expecting more. He'd gone onto his knees for this. How can he make her talk? She wants to let him know that having a baby has made him family, not a boyfriend or a lover. In just a couple of hours, she thinks, he'll be back at the bakery; let's do this properly.

"Who's in charge?" she says.

"I'm going back soon," he says, his forehead on the armrest where her arm had been.

"Someone has to be in charge," she says, fitting on the oven-glove.

"I don't trust them," he says.

She takes the tray of *kubbeh* from the oven, sets it down on the work counter, then warms up yesterday's saffron rice in the microwave oven. She tells herself not to fight, and holds Samih against her chest. Majid's coming up the four stairs from the conservatory, watching her move with the baby in one arm, as if the baby were still inside her, part of her, as if she could never fear dropping him.

"I could smell the *kubbeh* from the street," he says.

"Sit, sit," she says. "You must be starving."

"You're beautiful with the baby," he says.

Majid picks three *kubbeh* off the plate and dishes himself up some rice. Becka's getting bottles of lager from the fridge, wondering if love and passion can really just disappear like this, in seconds, without warning. Is it normal to hate so much? There was always passion. Especially passion: the way his hair lay on his forehead, the way his eyes made her think of Gypsies.

161

Anywhere but here, she thinks. Somewhere light and easy; to run on beaches, fly kites, have her arms free. She knows this woman who left her husband after 25 years, went to visit her brother in France and never came back. And another guy whose wife left him after eleven years. He was cooking their dinner, and she came downstairs with a suitcase in her hand, said she was going away for the weekend, and wanted him out by Monday. Becka wants to be back in the mango groves in the desert, lying on the damp lawn, late morning just after the sprinklers have been turned off, sunbathing. But she's in a strange country with a strange man and a baby stuck to her hip like a Siamese twin.

"Aren't you eating?" Majid says.

"My uncle Stuart died," Becka says, back at the counter, sliding a can of lager over to him and picking a *kubbeh* off the tray with her fingers as if she were dancing past a buffet counter. Keep going. She feels reckless, saying the word out loud like that; she could fly with Samih on her breast. The exhilaration of being able to say it like that. No preamble or euphemisms. For the first time to say: Stuart died.

Majid cuts off the edge of his *kubbeh* with a spoon and scoops it up with rice. He eats so elegantly, so precisely, she can't hate him for that one gesture that makes her want to be him. To watch a man who's been properly fed and cared for. That's when she knew she'd love him, when they stood together by the river eating Egyptian *ful* from paper plates and drinking the new Palestinian beer. She loves to cook for him, to see him relish his toast in the morning, spreading butter and blueberry jam. Now he's saying he doesn't know any Stuarts.

"Australia Stuart," she says. "My godfather."

"The one with the mad wife?" Majid says.

"My father's brother," she says.

162

"Where you close?" Majid says.

Majid always leans over his plate when he brings food to his mouth, as if everything could drip down the front of his shirt and onto his trousers. He puts a whole *kubbeh* in and kneads it against the insides of his cheeks before chewing. He frowns at her as if over the top of reading glasses, a soft frown, like she has unexpectedly become a stranger to him.

"Are you okay?" he says.

She can tell he wants to get up and hug her. She hates that word, hug, like some slug-like, engulfing creature. A slug hug. She also knows that if he had the courage to get up and hold her, she'd let him. She would cry on his shoulder, the baby nestled between them. It's nearly eight o'clock. Do something generous, she tells herself: love him, show him, let him in.

"I'm fine," she says. "Let's talk about other things."

"What did you do today?" he says.

"Cooked and fed," she says. "And then there was the news about Stuart."

"Is his wife still alive?" Majid says, unsure now what questions to ask.

"His wife?" she says. "The loony estate agent?"

"What kind of man was he?"

She remembers nothing; that's what she always tells herself, that way there is nothing to go back to, nothing to miss. Now is all that matters. Then today at noon, just as she's settling down with her baby, Shirls calls, this woman she barely knows, who tells her: "Your Uncle Stuart passed away two hours ago." Twenty years since she'd see him, since her bat-mitzvah and he'd come to Cape Town with Shirls before moving to Australia. In those years she'd finished school, finished college, gone to Israel for a while, now she was in London, teaching English to Hasidic women. Living a life like nobody's daughter.

"I don't remember much," she says.

"Did you love him?" Majid says.

"I think he was kind," she says. "I don't have bad memories of him."

She surprises herself. Her frown, a private, internal conversation. She doesn't trust herself to think such things. Majid smiles like she's just given him the present she's been keeping behind her back, shown him a possibility, again, something he sees in her when she holds their son.

"How's Samih been?" he asks.

"He's the best," she says.

"He's fast asleep."

"Stuart was the last South African, you know," Becka says.

"And there's you," he says.

"I'm the family's Holocaust survivor," she says.

She knows it's hard to keep up with her, to let her dictate the stopping and starting. For her, this is where the horror begins; opening up to love, exposed and unarmoured, then she has to hate someone to protect herself. Becka eats a small *kubbeh*, whole, drinks the last of her can, fills her mouth, washes it down. Where to from here? So, when Majid gets off his high stool and comes to kiss her, she turns to offer her cheek, not her mouth, which is pouting and closed, as if she were all gums.

"I'm smelly," she says. "I smell of frying and baby dribble."

"No, you don't," he says. "And so what? I smell of sweat and yeast."

Majid takes his plate to the sink to wash and she looks at his back, furtively, as if her gaze were a confession of weakness, the band of skin between his hairline and the collar of his T-shirt, as he puts the left-overs into a plastic container. She looks at him as if the answer might appear from the back of his neck. She's been trying to ignore his presence ever since the baby arrived. He doesn't always know this but his flesh does; and Becka knows him better than he knows himself.

"Your *kubbeh* is perfect," Majid says.

"Don't you have to get back," she says.

In Abney Park Cemetery the next day, the heat and the dense smell of foliage takes Becka back to the mango groves on the *moshav* in Israel. She'd been a volunteer first, staying on the *moshav* in a house abandoned by a couple who'd run away from their debts and gone to live in Canada. In the mornings, Becka and the others worked in the mango groves — most of them allergic to the violent pollen of mango blossoms — topless, using their T-shirts to blow their noses into.

Becka smiles at the memory, walking with Samih in a sling amongst the tombstones like rows of bad teeth. Ivy everywhere, and snowdrops at the edges of the footpaths. The tree tunnels and the dampness remind her of early mornings in the desert when the air is thick with dew, before the sun parches everything. Avigdor would wake them at five for hothouse duty, picking and packing roses for export. Then coffee and buttered rolls, which they ate in the shade at the side of the house where Avigdor bred snails for a French bistro in Tel Aviv. And in the afternoons, after lunch, they'd lie in the overgrown back garden, basking in the sun and reading Katherine Mansfield.

It was during these first days of unreal existence — picking mangoes, pruning roses, lying half-naked amongst desert weeds — that Avigdor suggested they do some work on the garden. She came as a volunteer and left as his lover, banished like Hagar, when his wife found out.

The rustling of leaves makes her turn, she'll show

165

Samih the squirrel; it'll be the first time: Look, Sam, a squirrel, she'll say, and a whole new world will open up. (But there I was, looking at her, and in front of me a man on his kneels with my cock in his mouth.) Samih feels his mother's heart jump and looks up for her eyes. The man on his knees gets up and fumbles with the buttons on his jeans, scurrying off into the bushes. Becka stands like a deer in headlights, thinking: Ooh, a squirrel. (My cock was now in full view, erect, as if — she told me later — I was expecting her to genuflect and take the kneeler's place.

"Nice day," I say, tucking my cock back in and pulling up my trousers.)

Becka smiles.

She's in London.

It's a lovely day.

"Nice penis," she says. "Was I interrupting something?"

"How do you do," he says. "I'm Dan."

First the accent, the recognition, then the towns they're from, the names, the Jewish geography — do you know...? do you know...? his mother went to school with mine; my adopted brother lives there now — a relief for both of them after years of England and trying to avoid just this kind of meeting. The coming together of identical biographies: Jewish schools, Habonim camp, a few years in Israel, and now London. It was a kind of homecoming, as if they might fall into each other's arms like long lost cousins from the Lithuanian gene mire of South Africa. When their differences start appearing it's a surprise and a comfort.

They'd been walking in the cemetery for an hour when Becka had to go, remembering that everything revolves around Samih. Both she and Dan have become cautious about suggesting tea, not to appear too eager, not to show how starved they are for home. But now she really has to go.

"Could you hold him for a bit?" she says.

She wants to trust this man, to believe their opening up is mutual. Becka needs to retie the sling; it's been slipping down her front, and her back aches.

"Let's sit down for a while," she says.

They settle on the lawn at the entrance to the cemetery in the company of some crusties and a couple of sleeping drunks. Dan sits on the grass and Becka kneels down and hands her baby to him.

The end of my family died yesterday, she wants to say, removing the sling from around her neck, but she keeps this knowledge to herself, like a stolen jewel, like money hard earned, to spend as she wishes, as she takes her baby back into her arms. And she listens to Dan talk about sex in the cemetery, a private public space where men approach each other for love and sex and friendship. There are days, he says, when it feels like home; a place where he's always welcome, where he can be sure there'll be someone to talk to, someone to be kissed by.

"And suck your thingie," she says, smiling.

This is what happens after they part: Dan calls and Becka can't make it. Eventually it all gets messy and it's Dan's fault, mainly. He'd hoped she wouldn't find out, that the three of them would find a way to accommodate what was happening. But Becka was the one who finally put a stop to it all; to Dan and her and to her and Majid.

(So for now, this is the only kind of story I can tell. A confession motivated by guilt; I want to be forgiven. Why, Becka says, so you can do it all again? He still loves you, I tell her. He loves you and I love you.)

When Becka and Samih get home from the cemetery, she can tell he needs changing without checking his nappy, so she lays him down on his back on the rug in the living room. What a beautiful body: the gorgeous folds of flesh around his knees and elbows; a perfect fat round baby

167

with wondrous fingers. "Who's just the most poifect baby?" Her lips against his stomach, warm ivory, his chest and transparent nipples all silk. She could eat him up. He's giggling, just like she taught him, making him chuckle when she blows kisses into his neck and cheeks. Mummy, I love you, he's saying, looking into the eyes that keep giving birth to him. He was made inside her; now she's responsible for his memories.

The pooh between his legs and on his bum smells sweet. She wipes around his penis, which is still bright red. Becka had agreed to circumcision as long as Majid held the baby; she didn't want Samih remembering her body as they sliced the skin off the top of his penis. She could have saved him; now he's bound to his people, which, she admits, fills her with wonder and gratitude. His umbilical cord has only just fallen off, a dry arrow-head, leaving small marks on his stomach where it chafed his skin. She'd hoped it wouldn't and had cut a slit in a breast pad, fed the cord and peg through the hole, and rested the drying flesh on the pad like a glass slipper.

"I think I've found you an uncle?" she says.

She chuckles into his mouth and kisses him. And when he's all clean and fresh, she sits crossed legged with him in her lap and feeds him. The living room looks out onto the street; though from where they sit on the floor all she sees are the roofs of the houses across the road. The man who'd sold them the house used to give yoga lessons on this floor, mats on the polished wood where now there's a thick rug. Once when Becka came to look at the house on her own, he was teaching, and the wife, now an ex-wife, showed her around and they sat in the kitchen whispering like school-girls. Her feet ache and Samih is asleep on her breast. She takes him upstairs to put him to sleep, which is where Majid finds them at three in the evening: Becka curled up in a ball and Samih wide awake, giggling at the ceiling.

THE SWEET THING

At a table at the back of Compton's Bar, Derek sat lost in thought. Outside it was a cold night, colder than it had been all winter; inside the music was loud: not the sort of music he'd listen to out of choice — Madonna, Steps, Kylie — still, it was the kind he enjoyed when he was getting drunk. He was also glad that it would soon be closing time and he'd be able to head on home. At the table next to his, a group of young muscle boys chatted away, and from time to time Derek would catch a word of their conversation, or a whiff of their after-shaves.

Mark, the owner of an old fringe theatre on Great Windmill Street, who lived in a flat nearby, was standing at the bar surveying the crowd.

"Enough of this," he cried in despair. "Enough drinking! It's always full of drunks in here. Horrible. It's Armageddon! Why don't you all go to the theatre? Go to an exhibition, go to the opera. Anything. Just stop all this drinking and fucking!"

Catching Derek's eye, he went on: "You sweet thing," he said. "I've seen you here before. But you don't look like a drunk. You're not like all these silly queens. What *are* you doing here?"

Mark came over to sit with Derek just as the gym boys were putting on their puffer jackets and getting ready to leave. They didn't like being near a man who couldn't lower his voice in a public place. Derek listened in silence as Mark went on and on, and he frowned and nodded and occasionally said "oh, really?" or "aha." In the end, Mark's deep unhappiness touched Derek and he agreed to go home with him. Mark was tall and skinny; his face was sallow and his long black hair was tucked behind his ears; he spoke in the nicotine voice of an aging movie star. He seemed troubled. Derek was falling in love.

Derek was always falling in love. He adored his mother when he was a boy; loved his uncle, who took him on hiking trips; and then he loved his Maths teacher, Mr Watson, who used to pinch the boys' legs when they got their sums wrong. Derek was a quiet and generous man with gentle eyes. When men looked at his dark stubble, his long thin neck with the scar, his rare, playful smile, that appeared when he was embarrassed, they thought: "I could trust you." When women saw the way Derek cared for their family members in the hospice where he worked, they would approach him at some point, shake his hand, and declare sincerely: "Oh, you're such a sweet thing."

Mark's flat, which he'd inherited from an uncle, a friend of Francis Bacon, was on Brewer Street around the corner from his theatre. In the evenings, lying in bed, even with the windows closed, they could hear people walking up and down the street, and Derek couldn't help but think: This is the heart of theatre history, and now, with Mark, I am part of it all. This thought excited him, and at night, after they'd had sex, he'd fight sleep just to stay awake and hear the comings and goings of patrons and actors, and when Mark came home late, drunk, from the theatre or the pub, Derek would leave the sheets draped around his waist, his torso uncovered for Mark to touch, then he would smile, and Mark would say "I knew you were awake," and Derek would let Mark fuck him.

Mark suggested Derek move in. And when he did, and had unpacked the few shirts and trousers he'd brought, Mark looked at his long neck with the scar, at his smooth torso, his generous eyes, free of cynicism and bitchiness, he said: "You are such a sweet thing."

Mark was as happy as his kind can get, though his theatre never really filled up and gay men kept drinking,

170

rather than going to the opera or an exhibition.

Derek and Mark enjoyed living together. Derek gave up his nursing job at the hospice in Clapham and helped Mark at the theatre. He worked in the box office, saw that the ushers had clean, ironed uniforms and all six flavours of ice cream; he kept an account of the expenses and paid the wages.

Derek would tell his friends that the theatre was the most exciting place to be and, really, he'd always wanted to be an actor, and that's why he was such a good nurse because he knew it was all a performance, and wasn't everything in life a performance, after all. And sometimes in the mornings, or after a show when the theatre was empty, Derek would walk out on stage and recite a few lines from the play that was showing at the time — *Cat on a Hot Tin Roof*, *Who's Afraid of Virginia Woolf?* — and take a bow, imagining the audience cheering, the seats full, the balcony overflowing. Derek was where he belonged.

And indeed, Derek had something to do with the gradual success of the theatre. He encouraged Mark to stage a musical every now and then, just to make the money he needed to put on the more serious plays — Tennessee Williams, Edward Albee — all of them with all-male casts, of course, for Mark insisted that that's how they'd originally been imagined.

"But do gay men care?" Derek would say to his friend Trish, his arms open as if he'd just been refused a hug by a young child. "All they care about is where the next drink or the next fuck is coming from. They're not interested in their heritage and culture. *This* is our history. Last week we had Hans Christian Andersen's fairy tales, and did anyone care that Andersen was gay? They have no pride, no sense of their own selves. But when we put on this musical nonsense they all pile in, singing along with the

171

actors. Next month we're doing *The Rape of Lucretia*. You must come and see it."

Like Mark, Derek criticised gay men for their shallowness and their ignorance. And whenever there was a nasty review in *Time Out* or *The Pink Paper*, he moped around the house, cried as if he'd just been insulted in public, then wrote a letter to the editor, demanding the theatre critic be sacked. The actors liked Derek; they nicknamed him Florence — for his nursing past, and for the flesh flowers and little bottles of mineral water he put in their dressing rooms. When they came off stage, there was always a warm drink waiting. They called him "a sweet thing" and would ask him for advice about love, or about various sexually transmitted diseases.

In January and February, having hired the theatre out for rehearsals to a small theatre company, Derek and Mark went to the South of France to spend some time in a villa. Derek was eating well, putting on weight, and enjoyed being taken care of by the young Algerian who cooked and cleaned for them. Mark drank more and more, and ranted about the decline of good theatre; he complained that nobody wrote plays anymore and that gay men were abandoning the beautiful things in life. At night, Derek made them hot chocolate, massaged Mark's back with lavender oil, his chest with eucalyptus, and then covered him in white cotton sheets.

"You darling," Mark would say, tears in his eyes, rubbing Derek's tummy. "You're such a sweet thing."

One year, soon after they got back to London, Mark went to Paris to audition actors for a new production of *Our Lady of the Flowers*; Derek found the flat big and empty and the noises outside felt like thieves trying to break in. They kept him awake at night, so he sat at the window and watched people walking up and down Brewer Street, and with the window open, the smell of roasting peanuts from a nearby restaurant would waft in and calm him. And even though he knew Mark had only gone for a couple of weeks, on nights like these he felt like Solveig or Penelope, all the women who spent years waiting for their lovers.

Mark called to say he'd be away for another week; he'd only found a couple of actors who could read the English text. He asked Derek to oversee the upcoming musical. But late one night, when Derek was dreaming about his role in *The Seagull*, the phone rang, and, Derek wondered in the dream, whether there were phones in those days, or whether it was coming from back stage; its persistence woke him at 4.23am, two days before Mark was due home.

"Can I speak with Derek," said a man with a strong French accent.

Derek imagined Mark's French lover, or the father of a young man he'd seduced. He always suspected Mark was using his trips abroad to sleep with other men, or maybe he had a lover he'd meet with in these places. Derek shook while the man told him: "Big accident. Mark, he is in big accident."

That was what the man said — *aksi-dah* — and Derek imagined the car crashing into Mark as he walked, drunk, across the road near the wooden foot-bridge that led from the Louvre back onto the Left Bank.

"My poor baby," Derek sobbed. "My dear Mark. Why did I ever listen to you at that silly bar? Why did I ever fall in love with you? What will I do now? What will I do without you?"

Derek arranged for Mark to be cremated in Paris and sneaked into Pere Lachaise with his ashes, sprinkling them around the graves of every playwright and actor he could find. When Derek got back to London with just a tablespoon of Mark's ashes in the urn, he lay down on their bed and cried, his sadness filling him.

173

Two months later when Derek was returning home from the theatre, it so happened that another well-known Soho figure and friend of Mark's, Andrew Earnest, was on his way home, having been to see Barbara Cook do Sondheim at the Lyric. Andrew was the author of several gay romance novels, though with his Mohican haircut, knee-length herring-bone coat, and the multiple studs in his ears, he looked more like a punk than a distinguished writer.

"There is no reason for death," he said, after he and Derek had hugged. "There's no such actuality as fate, no natural order of things. I've lost so many friends and lovers. No-one's meant to die, but we do. We must live like gods and wait for death."

They hugged again at Derek's door, said goodbye, and Andrew carried on to his flat on Dean Street. All night Andrew's deep, concerned voice filled Derek's head, and as he was drifting off to sleep the diamonds in Andrew's ears became stars in the sky, and a bright white ship drifted into the sunset. Derek was falling in love. Apparently he'd made an impression on Andrew, because when Derek bumped into Tom from the gay bookshop and they went for coffee, the first thing Tom mentioned was Andrew Earnest's new book.

"He's this country's greatest literary voice," Tom said.

According to Tom, Andrew was a serious and committed man, dependable, adventurous, and solvent. And if he, Tom, didn't have Mustafa, he'd have snapped Andrew up ages ago. Three days later, Derek received an invitation to the launch of Andrew's new book at the Groucho. Derek was already in love, and in the week leading up to the event he tossed and turned in bed as if creditors were breathing down his neck. The night of the launch Derek went home with Andrew, and a few weeks later he moved in.

Derek set up Mark's flat as a residence for visiting actors and directors. He and Andrew lived happily together. Andrew wrote in his study all morning and afternoon, and would wear a shark's tooth on a chain around his neck to indicate he was not to be disturbed. Derek would answer the phone when he wasn't at the theatre, which he eventually sold to someone who sold it to a theatre mogul. Derek wasn't sure what Mark would have to say about the selling off of his theatre; he was also too busy to ponder this question. He organised book-signing trips for Andrew; called up publishers in America to get them to bring out new editions of his books; and he volunteered once a week at the gay bookshop, which was really an opportunity to promote Andrew's books and to talk to Tom, the customers, and to his friend Trish, about writing.

"The imagination works hardest when confronted with the written word," Derek would tell them. "Out of all artists, writers put the most imaginative energy into their work, they are the true creators, bringing worlds into being out of nothing. You can't imagine the concentration needed to write, and the silence," he said, lifting his palm to the heavens, then slapping his forehead, as if this was the cross he had to bear. "Oh, the silence."

Derek felt he'd been amongst writers all his life, and that indeed the whole of civilisation depended on more books being written. He felt comforted when he heard words like author, publish, writer, chapter, pen, ink, paper. At night, he'd dream about manuscripts neatly tied with red ribbons being carried by messengers in gold and green uniforms to the royal printing press; he'd dream about dancers with pens for legs who'd write poetry with the tips of their toes, gracefully and passionately, until they filled the world with words and no-one could tell one country from the next and people wondered about trying to unravel themselves from webs of blue ink. Derek would wake up with a start and Andrew would say to him tenderly:

"What the matter, my sweet thing? Come, let me hug you."

Andrew's ideas were Derek's ideas. If he thought that some writer was sanitary and middle class and behaved like a heterosexual in his writing, then Derek thought the same. Andrew didn't like going on holiday, not the way Mark enjoyed being in foreign cities; he preferred to get on with his writing, or review a book for *The Independent*. Derek lost interest in travel, and stayed home to read over the summer holidays, and Christmas, and Easter and Passover.

"You're always at home or in a fucking bookshop," Trish said to him. "What happened to late nights at the pub, getting pissed, telling horror stories about dying patients. You need to get out more; let's go to a movie, or to Heaven. Fuck it, let's go to the opera."

"We don't have time for that," Derek replied. "We have to worry about the muse. The muse doesn't like getting drunk or having to sit around watching the kind of shit that passes for theatre nowadays. Time's too precious when there are books to be written."

One Saturday Andrew came home and told Derek he was sick. The cough he'd had for the past ten days was AIDS-related and he was going into hospital for a while. The doctors wanted to put him through some tests; make sure the cough didn't develop into pneumonia. They sat on the couch in the living room holding hands, a grave expression on their faces. They drank tea and Derek made them a meal of pasta with cream and Emental and fresh nutmeg. When Andrew was in hospital, Derek took him food every day: rice and peas like a Jamaican friend had taught him to make; spinach and chickpea soup with lots of lemon; or a take-away from Andrew's favourite Malaysian restaurant on Great Windmill Street. Andrew came back home and they'd go once a week to the alternative health centre for shiatsu massages and Reiki. Andrew had an acupuncturist. Derek didn't fancy having needles stuck into him.

"Cock is about all I can manage," he said to Trish.

It was harder to joke with Andrew; he was getting weaker and weaker. When Andrew was away in hospital, and even when he was at home, Derek would lie awake at night and cry. "But we were so happy," he said to himself, incredulous at the amount of sorrow he had to bear. With AIDS came a buddy, Colin, a young man social services had assigned to Andrew. Colin would turn up with his dog, then clean the house, prepare roast chicken and potatoes, and sit at Andrew's bedside telling him stories, and the three of them would sometimes play games, silly games, to take Andrew's mind off the pain. When Andrew fell asleep, Derek and Colin would sit in the kitchen and Colin would tell him about his sex life, which both fascinated and disturbed Derek.

Colin had once been married and had a daughter called Trudy. He'd left his wife soon after he came out; she'd introduced him to his first lover. Now they were good friends and often met up to go to the theatre, or to take their daughter to one of the theme parks outside London. Derek felt lucky to know such a kind and generous man.

"Now tell me a sex story, too," Derek would say, getting up to make another pot of tea. "Where are you off to tonight? I don't know how you do it. Aren't you scared? I think I'm a bit jealous."

Derek always spoke with kindness, no hint of the judgmental tone he'd hear in everything Mark used to say about gay men and their compulsive behaviours. Colin's stories about backrooms and parks and meeting men over the phone and the internet, and going off to parts of London Derek had never even heard of, smacked of freedom and the exhilaration of being accountable to no-one.

"Some angel must be looking after you," Derek said, putting the mugs in the sink and excusing himself to check on Andrew.

After Colin had left — to take his dog for a walk in Russell Square — Derek would sit by Andrew's bed, and if he was awake he'd tell him in a low voice about Colin's sexual activities, and both of them, out of a mixture of delight and sadness would laugh out loud, and use that opportunity to share more of their own sexual history with each other. On days when Andrew felt stronger they'd have sex, sometimes pretending to be in a dingy darkroom, in the bushes on the Heath, or in a hotel: Derek was room service, well-mannered and compliant, and Andrew was a demanding guest.

Derek and Andrew continued to live in fear and good humour for another three years. But one winter in Zurich, where a book of Andrew's had just been translated into German, Andrew got a cold on a day when the sky was blue and they'd been skating on a small lake just outside the city. The doctors did what they could, and when he got back to London, and his body wouldn't respond to medication, he died at home two weeks later. Derek was alone again.

"Oh, my sweetheart, what will I do now?" he cried, after burying Andrew in the Jewish cemetery in Finchley. "How will I go on without you? I don't have anyone in the world now that you're gone."

Derek wore white. He'd read somewhere — maybe in one of Andrew's books — that this was the Jewish colour of mourning. He gave their old clothes to the Crusaid charity shop. Colin took the boxes there in his van. Derek seldom left the house, except to visit Andrew's grave, or to take a day trip to Brighton, where he'd walk along the beach-front and sit on a bench facing the sea until the sun set; he went for days without speaking to anyone. It was a year before he went out and bought himself a colourful sweatshirt and a pair of denim jean; he had Andrew's flat painted — each room a different colour — yellow, blue, and terra-cotta red.

Sometimes he'd talk to people he knew on the street, but very few of them came to the flat, so no-one really knew how he was. Andrew's friends, who'd pop round to invite him to their launches and exhibitions, more out of loyalty to Andrew than anything else, and others who'd bump into Derek walking Colin's dog in St James' Park, put two and two together and guessed there was something going on between him and the buddy. And then there were the things he'd say, which sealed it for his friend Trish, and anyone else who'd known him for a while.

"I'm centering myself," Derek said. "My chi's been all wrong for such a long time. All my chakras have to be realigned."

He was repeating Colin's ideas and had the same opinion as him about everything. Clearly, he could not live for very long without some attachment; now he'd found happiness in this New Age radical faerie. No-one condemned Derek for this, no-one ever thought badly of him; he was a sweet thing. Neither he nor Colin talked about the change in their relationship; they tried to keep it a secret, but Derek, when he went with Colin to the Buddhist Centre, or to an evening of 5-Rhythms Dance, would talk about chakras and self-discovery, negative energy and the importance of meditation, and on their way home, walking up Southampton Row and turning left onto Bloomsbury Way, heading towards Dean Street, Colin said to Derek:

"You have to find your own voice. You can't keep

repeating what you hear me say. I've been searching for years, I've used my experiences, my past, got in touch with my authentic desires in order to discover what my true voice is. You have to look back at what you've gone through, see where you've been, what you've done, who you've loved and been loved by, and work out where *you* want to go, what *you* want to think."

Derek would smile at Colin and rest his head on his shoulder: "I do mean what I say, my darling," and he'd frown, concerned. "You're not angry at me, are you?"

The happiness Derek felt came to an abrupt end when Colin decided to move to a Buddhist retreat in Devon, miles from anywhere, with no access to a telephone, and a vow of silence for the first three months. He asked Derek to look after his dog, and when Derek agreed, Colin brought her food-bowl and sleeping-basket to the flat, and left for Devon the next day.

Now Derek was alone again. His parents had long been dead and the only family he had, distant cousins from a great-aunt on his mother's side, ran a furniture empire in Australia. Derek began to put on weight and started balding; men no longer looked at him in the streets, and those who did, the short little skinny ones, didn't interest him; women no longer smiled at him. He was getting old, he told Trish, he had no-one, and now all that was left for him to do was get through the days, bear the grief, and hope for a pain-free death.

Sometimes he'd walk past the Theatre, and he'd watch the people — mainly tourists from America and Japan — coming out of a performance, putting on their coats, swapping their impressions of the play, usually in no more than a word or two, and hurry off to hail a cab. Derek would walk into bookshops to leaf through copies of Andrew's books, lingering on the photo on the inside back cover, sometimes reading the bits about Tony the doctor who'd gone off to Croatia, a character Andrew had based on Derek. All Derek wanted was to have Mark and Andrew back; he didn't want love, he didn't want sympathy, and he certainly didn't want sex. He watched the good-looking men of Soho with indifference, and when he got home he'd heat up some soup and eat it with thick slices of bread and butter; then he'd go to bed and dream about graveyards and gaunt Sophia Lorens with Cockney accents, or about meeting an ex-lover in the desert who was on his way to his honeymoon. Derek woke up disappointed — at his dreams, and at the prospect of another day.

Worst of all was that he didn't know what to think. He had no opinions about anything. Yes, he saw things and understood them, but he didn't have anything to say; besides, there wasn't anyone to say anything to anyway. He'd see beggars on the pavement outside his flat, hear about the conflict in the Middle East, watch so-and-so win an Oscar, and still he wasn't sure what he thought about it all. When he was with Mark and Andrew, or even when he spent time with Colin, he knew what he thought, he had opinions; now there was only loss and sadness and a huge void that had opened up inside him that could never be filled.

Soho was changing. There seemed to be more sex shops, and gay men were more muscled than ever. Derek grew lonelier in the flat on Dean Street, and the new colours on the walls were more of an affront than a source of pleasure. Winters seemed longer, and when spring came and young tourists poured into the city and men removed more layers of clothing, Derek realised how fat he'd become, how difficult it was to keep up with the dog when he took her for walks. In St James' Park, he'd be overcome with memories of Mark and Andrew — the summer evening he and Mark had walked home drunk from a party in Kensington and Mark had got up onto the bandstand and recited a love poem by Rumi, and the year Andrew got ill and they'd come to sit by the pond with cake and tea in styrofoam cups and watch the ducks — and Derek would be filled with a melancholy that was both sustaining and crippling and tears blurred his vision, and then the dog would tug on her lead and Derek would be jerked out of his gloom and pulled along. When Derek let the dog off her lead, she would bark as an invitation to play, and mostly Derek remained unmoved — he wanted a man to consume him completely, not a canine substitute — but the dog's joy was infectious.

"Okay, dog," he said. "If you want to run, we'll run."

And Derek broke into a sprint and the dog barked at his side, egging him on, and Derek's chest felt like it would cave in on itself, but he kept going and his lungs opened up and he ran and coughed and ran and the cool spring air invigorated him. And so it happened day after day, the joy of running in the park, Derek would look forward to the afternoon when he would take the dog for a walk. The days were getting longer and warmer and the park was filling up with people, some of whom turned as Derek ran past; the men to admire, the women to smile, the children to enjoy the sight of a laughing man and a big brown happy barking dog.

Late in the afternoon one hot July day as Derek was coming home from the park, sweating, the dog panting at his heels, someone was waiting on the stairs outside his flat. Derek stopped in his tracks. It was Colin, his hair tied back in a ponytail, his beard lush and thick, and a cream cotton shirt open down to his bellybutton, his lovely chest hair a temptation. Derek hoped he wouldn't start crying, but he did, and they hugged and Colin's smell brought everything back to him. He was so excited he couldn't remember later how he'd opened the front door, or whether he'd taken a shower while Colin made them mugs of tea.

"So, dear friend," Derek said, trying not to shake. "What brings you back to dirty noisy old London?"

"This is where I want to live," Colin said. "In all those months of silence I realised how much I really love people, I love them, and I've decided to live here in the heart of Soho and teach people about the source of creativity, and how to get in touch with their own well of inventiveness. Besides, the time has come for my daughter to live with me. That was the agreement we made when my wife and I separated. Trudy's nine; I think she's looking forward to coming to live with me."

"Have you found a flat?" Derek said.

"Still looking," Colin said. "But I will. I'll find one very soon."

"Why not move into Mark's flat? It's a great place to live, and you'll only need to pay the bills." Derek was so excited he thought he might cry. "You could live there with Trudy; there's a room for each of you and a spare one for guests. It'll be great to have you living in the neighbourhood."

The next day Derek got someone in to paint Mark's flat, and while the man painted, Derek planted new bulbs in the window boxes that had been empty for years and were covered in soot. He bought a new sofa and an armchair, a nice big soft one; he was planing to read bedtime stories to Trudy. His whole body seemed to become lighter; he smiled more and joined a gym. It was as if he'd been kissed by a prince.

Colin moved into Mark's flat and with him came Trudy, a tall, vibrant young girl with long curly brown hair and dimples, and an expression that managed to contain both a smile and a frown, a bemused expression Derek recognised as Colin's. She brought with her a toy bunny called Rover, all threadbare and with only one eye. What with the dog jumping around and Trudy's inquisitiveness, and Colin's excitement, not to mention the cartwheels Derek was doing inside, the place was abuzz with energy.

"Did you live here when you were little?" Trudy asked. "Did you live here with your mummy and your daddy?"

Derek explained the history of the flat and promised that one day they'd go for a walk and he'd show her the theatre that belonged to Mark. Later that night, after her bath, Trudy came into the living to say goodnight to Uncle D, as she called him.

"Goodnight, my sweet thing," Derek said. "You're going to be very happy here. I just know it. There's lots of exciting things to do around here."

"My daddy's a bisexual," Trudy said.

"Oh, you are clever," said Derek. "Did your daddy tell you that?"

"He has sex with men and he had sex with my mummy," she said. "Are you a bisexual?"

And although Derek had wanted to say, no, my sweet thing, Uncle D loves your daddy, he said: "I'm gay" and thought it strange that this was the first time he'd come out to a nine-year old, and how frightening and liberating it was, as if he too were nine again and didn't have to hide from the world. "No, my sweet, I'm not bisexual; I'm gay."

It was like starting all over again, like being born into honesty.

"Okay," said Trudy. "Goodnight, Uncle D."

"Goodnight, sweetheart," Derek said.

Colin stood in the doorway, smiling, his T-shirt still wet from washing Trudy's hair: "Come on, young lady," he said. "It's time for bed."

Trudy went to a nice private school not far from the flat with a cosmopolitan group of pupils and a head teacher who believed in a liberal education and the glory of social-ism. Trudy learnt about the Russian Revolution and came home to tell them about Lenin and Marx and about the horrid Stalin who sent lots of people to camp where it was freezing cold.

Two years later, in January, when the pavements were white with snow and the sky a bright blue — on a day not unlike the one Andrew had caught his cold on — it was time for Trudy to go back to her mother. Colin asked Derek to move in with him, so Derek suggested Trudy and her mum move into the flat on Dean Street, which they agreed to. Derek still spent time with Trudy.

"Tell me your life story," Trudy said to Derek one evening after he'd made dinner for the two of them. Colin was running a workshop at The Healing Centre, his ex-wife was working late at the theatre, and Derek and Trudy had spent the day at the V&A, then shopping on Regent's Street, then dinner, a bath, and now a story.

"My life's not very interesting," Derek said.

"Then make it up," Trudy said. "I don't mind."

"Well, then, let's see," Derek said. "Once upon a time there was a prince called…"

"Uncle Derek," said Trudy.

"There was a prince called Uncle Derek who kept falling in love."

"Has it got a happy ending?" said Trudy.

"Of course it has," said Derek. "Now can I carry on?"

Also available from Five Leaves

The Smug Bridegroom
by Robert Hamberger

A collection of deeply personal poems by a writer who has a wonderful way of reconciling the anecdotal and the rhetorical. His writing traces the shifts in family life and relationships, the break up of marriage and the renewal of hope, which is itself endangered by heart surgery. The collection includes Robert Hamberger's long sonnet sequence, The Rule of Earth. Robert Hamberger was one of the 2005 "Alt Gen" poets.

Robert Hamberger writes in a deceptively simple manner. A must for poetry readers and a perfect introduction for the curious. **GAY TIMES**

The Rule of Earth is a collection of exquisite sonnets about a gay relationship that moved me to tears. To be honest, I've often seen the sonnet as a kind of straightjacket in the wrong hands, but Hamberger makes them fly. **IAN MCMILLAN**

76 pages, 0907123880, £6.99

Flood Warning
by Berta Freistadt

These poems are about the melancholy and madness of love, celebrating love between women. The second part of the collection works on the question of identity, the making of community and the struggle of a London Jew to understand the war in Israel.

35 pages, 0907123945, £4.50

From bookshops, or, post free, from Five Leaves, PO Box 81, Nottingham NG5 4ER